D1061335

The Seagull & the Urn

Allison Bohl DeHart

SHOME DASGUPTA lives in Lafayette, LA. He is the author of *i am here And You Are Gone* (Winner of the 2010 OW Press Fiction Chapbook Contest) and *Tentacles, Numbing* (Black Coffee Press, 2013). His stories and poems have appeared in *Puerto Del Sol, New Orleans Review, NANO Fiction, Everyday Genius, Redivider, Magma Poetry*, and elsewhere. His fiction has been selected to appear in the *&Now Awards 2: The Best Innovative Writing* (&Now Books, 2013) and his work has been featured as a storySouth Million Writers Award Notable Story, nominated for the Best of the Net and longlisted for the Wigleaf Top 50. He is at *shomedome.com*.

The Seagull
&
the Urn

SHOME DASGUPTA

HarperCollins *Publishers* India

First published in India in 2013 by
HarperCollins *Publishers* India

Copyright © Shome Dasgupta 2013
Illustrations copyright © Arijit Ganguly 2013

ISBN: 978-93-5029-635-6

2 4 6 8 10 9 7 5 3 1

HarperCollins *Publishers*
A-53, Sector 57, Noida, Uttar Pradesh 201301, India
77-85 Fulham Palace Road, London W6 8JB, United Kingdom
Hazelton Lanes, 55 Avenue Road, Suite 2900, Toronto, Ontario M5R 3L2
and 1995 Markham Road, Scarborough, Ontario M1B 5M8, Canada
25 Ryde Road, Pymble, Sydney, NSW 2073, Australia
31 View Road, Glenfield, Auckland 10, New Zealand
10 East 53rd Street, New York NY 10022, USA

Typeset in 10/14 Goudy Old Style at
SÜRYA

Printed and bound at
Thomson Press (India) Ltd

For Mommy and Daddy.

Thank you for always loving me and supporting me, no matter how many times I mess up. Your encouragement has no boundaries—I am forever grateful.

1

MARCH WAS BORN IN THE MIDDLE OF APRIL. THE morning of her birthday was rainy, but by the evening the rain had stopped and the sun could be seen setting. She was born in the period of the waning rain and sun. The hospital was a small one, only a year old. Funded by a prominent local family, the Medallions, it was built after the death of their child, Ney. The town of Kolkaper was bordered by the Bay of Bengal on the east coast, Hyderabad was west of the city, Chennai to the south, while the Cave Forest lined the northern and western edges.

There were two causes for the death of Ney: she had caught pneumonia as she was received from Francesca's womb at the Medallion Mansion, and once she had entered the world with that sickness, the hospital refused to take her in. Ney's life was brief but momentous, because the events leading from her birth up to her passing laid the path for the wonderful life of March.

When the Medallions took Ney to the hospital, Dr Frez was stubborn and bitter. He held a grudge against the Medallions, particularly Nirana.

'We have the right to refuse business to any customer,' Dr Frez said.

Two years before the birth of Ney, Nirana and Dr Frez were involved in a lawsuit. The doctor had sued Nirana for being healthy, because he never needed to go to the hospital for treatment. When Dr Frez was just becoming a doctor, Nirana had assured him that he would be one of the hospital's best customers. However, due to the healthy and well-nourished life that Nirana was living, he never had cause to go to the hospital until the birth of his daughter. The case was faulty; it was clear that Dr Frez's insanity was increasing. Years and years devoted to his profession in medicine had eroded his rationality. He confused needles with noodles, crutches with stilts and, at one point, he thought a stethoscope was a dinosaur.

He insisted that the Medallions were nothing but a parasite's parasite. Nirana wanted no part of the case. He knew of Frez's insanity, and he didn't want to cause any further damage to the doctor's health. However, when the doctor claimed that the Medallions' ancestors lived lives full of cheating and stealing, Nirana had enough and he took the matter to court.

'He can say anything about me,' Nirana said. 'But my ancestors, and my ancestors' ancestors, they have nothing to do with this.'

The judge ruled in Nirana's favour, citing that, 'It is not Nirana's duty to become ill under any obligation.'

Frez never forgave Nirana. Ney's sickness was the first time since the lawsuit that the Medallions had gone to his hospital.

After denying the baby admission, Frez realized the injustice he was committing and rushed out of the hospital to call back the Medallions. 'Please, come back; the expenses shall be paid from my own salary,' he said. 'Within my insanity, there exists a small measure of rationality.'

The Medallions hurried back to the hospital. But as they placed Ney in the emergency room, she died from a sneeze.

'Achoo,' Ney said.

She had closed her eyes to sneeze and they never opened again.

Dr Frez could not look the Medallions in the eye. He put his hands on top of his head. He stuck his tongue out. He tried to speak, but nothing came out.

Without a word, Nirana and Francesca returned home. They were quiet during the drive back in the carriage. The driver whispered to the horses to be gentle. When they arrived at the mansion, Francesca was the first to speak.

'I must dream of my baby,' she said.

Ney was their first baby. Francesca spent the day in her room crying over the pure white cloths given to them by her friends to serve as bed sheets for the crib. Francesca's tears dissolved the sheets and there was nothing left but sorrow.

Nirana took time off from his work as a lawyer to console his wife. The citizens of Kolkaper made a pact to not commit any crimes or break any laws as long as Nirana was not working.

'This is no time for crime,' one thug said.

'We will show our enemies their due respect,' another thug said.

'How can we steal when there is no one to challenge us?' a reputable criminal said.

Those Nirana had sent to jail by successfully prosecuting them in court expressed their condolences. Jay – a man who was convicted of stealing the roots of trees and selling them in the black market as ancient elephant tusks – sent Nirana a card. And Brie-Logan, who had instigated the Great Bar Fight of the Century, had one of his cronies send the Medallions a crate of liquor and cheese.

Frez never forgave himself for the death of Ney. Seven days after her death, when no one was hospitalized, he gave the other workers the day off and locked himself in the same emergency room where Ney had passed away. He poured a bucket of gasoline all over the room and over himself. Before he had even lit a match, the heat from his own guilt caused a spark, setting him on fire. It eventually spread throughout the hospital, burning the building down. Ney was the last patient to have died under Frez's care. On the same day as Frez's fiery guilt, seven days after Ney's sneeze, the Medallions cremated their baby. The ashes were thrown into the ocean.

'She will have quite a journey,' Francesca said.

'An ash to each corner of the world and beyond,' Nirana said.

As they returned to their mansion, they saw the burning hospital and ran to the site, which was already surrounded by the townspeople, including the police and the firefighters.

'Frez has burnt himself to death and he has taken his whole life with him,' Francesca said.

'It wasn't his fault, though,' Nirana said. 'There was nothing that could have been done. A sneeze is a sneeze.'

They stood there until the sun set over the ocean and watched the last trails of smoke make their way into the sky.

'Poor man,' Francesca said. 'He always wanted to do right. And though he tried, things never went the way he wanted. Unnecessary guilt. We should have asked him over and told him that everything will be okay.'

'I now realize the pain he must have been carrying this past week,' Nirana said. 'It is our fault he died.'

'Too many deaths,' Francesca said.

The others had left for their nightly activities. But the Medallions remained until the last of the smoke disappeared and then went back to their home.

SOON AFTER THE ASHES OF NEY AND DR FREZ WERE RELEASED into the sky, Nirana met with his financial advisor, Chek. Nirana had a plan that he had come up with in his sleep the night before. They were to meet at the mansion. The smell of curry and vegetable soup filled its rooms as Chek knocked on the oak door. Chek and Nirana were childhood friends. They had gone to the same schools, from elementary school to their college years.

'Smells delicious,' Chek said. 'Let us skip this meeting and eat these savoury, scented foods.'

'Your appetite hasn't changed,' Nirana said. 'And I hope that it will always remain the same.'

In a sudden change of mood, Chek turned towards Nirana. 'My condolences to you and Francesca.'

Francesca met them in the foyer, known as the Pablo Hall, because its walls were filled with an assortment of Pablo Picasso's paintings, including *Guernica* and *The Old Man and His Guitar*. Chek hugged Francesca and whispered his condolences to her. Francesca kissed him on the cheek.

'Now, hurry and finish this business you all have to attend to and let us eat,' she said.

'It shouldn't take too long,' Nirana said. 'Come Chek, we will talk in my office.'

They walked through the foyer and living room, and into the office. Chek noticed the change in decoration and that the walls had been re-painted since he had last been there.

'This is wonderful,' he said.

'We've been trying to keep ourselves busy,' Nirana said. 'We thought that changing the look of the house would help us cope.'

Nirana sat behind his marble desk and Chek sat opposite him, the folders held underneath his arm. Nirana lit a cigar and offered one to Chek.

'I've stopped smoking since the hospital burned down,' Chek said.

'You are wise,' Nirana said. 'I've started smoking since the hospital burned down.'

Nirana pulled out a folder from the drawer.

'I want to fund the building of the new hospital, in memory of both Ney and Frez. It will be dedicated to them both. I wish the lawsuits had not come in the way of our friendship. Our family knew Frez for years. We tried, Chek, we tried to keep the relationship, but he would have none of it.'

'A shame,' Chek replied. 'Good health and insanity.'

'In his memory and hers, I would like to fund the new hospital for Kolkaper.'

'I knew you would want to. A ghost in my dream last night told me so.'

'A ghost?'

'It was a seagull,' Chek said. 'Flying with an urn in its mouth.'

'The seagull,' Nirana said.

He looked up at the ceiling – his eyes shone as he envisioned seabirds and seagulls and hawks and falcons swirling around the room. The ceiling itself turned into a seagull in Nirana's eyes. Chek tapped him on the shoulder, then called out his name and gave him a slight slap on the back. Nirana shook his head.

'Sorry,' Nirana said. 'I was remembering another world full of birds.'

'This morning, I checked your financial situation and you are in excellent condition.'

'I will then talk to the City Council tomorrow. And make all the arrangements. Will you be able to come?'

'We will go there together,' Chek said.

'Dinner,' Nirana said.

Nirana told Francesca about the new hospital and she smiled for the first time since the death of Ney.

THE NEXT DAY, NIRANA, CHEK AND THE CITY COUNCIL MET before noon. The Council office was made of oak and marble. There was a long table in the middle of the room, where the Council members sat and smoked cigars. There were pitchers of water at each end of the table and one in the middle. The head of the Council, Rinja, was happy to hear that the Medallions wanted to build a new hospital and they graciously accepted the offer.

'We would love to assist in your funding,' Rinja said.

His eyes were wide and watery. His moustache bobbed up and down as he talked. He rubbed his arms and looked at the pitchers of water.

'This will be the greatest hospital in Kolkaper.'

His eyebrows, two thick black caterpillars, lifted towards the sky.

'We hope it will be one of the best, but it will be hard without Dr Frez as part of the team,' Nirana said.

'He was one of the best,' Chek said.

'Too true,' Rinja replied. 'We will find a worthy replacement.'

They shook hands and construction began a week later. Nirana worked extra hours to make up for the neglect of his clients during the past few weeks. The thugs, who had been patient for so long, prepared to commit crimes again – there was stealing and robbing and vandalism. They were happy that Kolkaper's best lawyer had returned to work.

'We feel like we are back home again,' one thug said.

Francesca took up her childhood pastime of watercolour painting. She painted Ney and her husband, she painted their house and their garden. She painted the city and the seabirds and things she hadn't seen before – dreams of other worlds and other lives. She volunteered to work with various organizations in Kolkaper, such as the Department of Parks and Ducks, The Home for Children Without Homes and The Committee to Oversee the Blind. Francesca was a kind woman, who cared for those less fortunate than her. She always kept frozen chocolates in her purse so that she had something to give the beggars of Kolkaper when she went to the markets.

'With chocolate, they will realize the sweetness of the world, they must have had too much of its sour counterpart,' Francesca would say to her friends.

With diligent workers and sunny, clear weather, the new hospital was finished within six months. And in the time that the city didn't have a hospital, the people of Kolkaper had made a pact to not do anything dangerous – no one rode on skateboards or played rugby or sang in the rain. The thugs, though they had started to commit crimes again, kept their illegal activities to simple acts, nothing that involved fighting or shooting. No one needed any medical attention, except for Aurra, who was ninety-seven years old.

'I will wait till the hospital is finished and then I will die,' she told the house doctor. 'I will be the hospital's first baby.'

The hospital was small, but lavish. Each room had a painting either by de Kooning or Seurat. The walls were light blue. The floors were made of marble and children stared at the swirls of colour as they waited in the lobby. In the courtyard, there were a series of African tribal artworks, consisting of wooden, bronze and stone statues. There was a café, serving coffee and vegetables and for those who wished to eat unhealthy, there was a range of foods high in cholesterol.

'If I'm going to eat unhealthy,' one patient said, 'then I should eat unhealthy in the finest hospital of Kolkaper.'

4

SIX MONTHS AFTER THE HOSPITAL WAS BUILT, MARCH WAS born just outside it. The Faccinises weren't expecting this birth. Jonas, the father of the baby and husband to Maria, didn't know that his wife was pregnant. Maria didn't know she was pregnant either. Nine months ago, Jonas had to travel across the ocean for an important job dealing with metals. The night before he left, Jonas and Maria said their farewells and March was conceived. Maria, in her pining for Jonas, had slept for the nine months that he was not there, only waking up once to make sure the house was not on fire. The day Jonas returned from overseas, Maria opened her eyes.

'I could smell the dirt on your skin as soon as you entered Kolkaper,' she whispered.

Maria burped and felt the baby in her stomach. 'I must be pregnant,' she said.

'To the hospital,' Jonas said.

'Let us get as far as possible,' she replied.

They hurried toward the hospital, making frequent stops in the rain to see if she was about to give birth to a baby. They made it just short of their destination. Maria couldn't make it all the way up the stairs of the building. Jonas left her there and ran inside to get help. He found two doctors and three nurses, but as they rushed outside, just before the sun had set, Maria gave birth to March.

In the hospital room, Jonas caressed Maria's hair. She had slept for nine months, but she was a light sleeper, and her hair was kempt and combed; not one strand was out of place. She wore wrinkle-free-clothes, like they had just been taken out of the dresser drawer, folded and ironed.

'Rest. I will go and see March now.'

'I have rested for nine months. Let me go with you.'

Jonas helped her out of bed, and they walked to March's room. She was the Faccinises' first baby, as well as the hospital's first birth. They met Dr Slide on their way to the room.

'There appears to be a problem with the newborn,' he said.

'Can she already talk?' Jonas asked.

'She can't sleep. Her eyes have yet to close.'

They walked into March's room and saw her in a small wooden crib. She was on her back, her eyes open, staring at the ceiling.

'She should be sleeping. Her eyes should close at least

for a little bit. Since she has left Maria's stomach, she has done nothing but look around.'

'Are there any signs of ill health?' Maria asked.

'No, but this situation is unexplainable. She should be crying and sleeping and crying and sleeping.'

'Is she human?' Jonas asked.

'She has every human feature, from heartbeat to mucus.'

'What should we do?' Maria asked.

'We'll keep her here for a few days and see what happens, if that is okay with you. We may perform some tests.'

'We will stay here while you're conducting the tests,' Jonas said.

They stayed there for two days while March was put through a number of machines. A committee came and observed her, but they could find nothing wrong.

March didn't close her eyes to sleep. She was healthy, she was fed properly, her bowel movements were proper and her limbs were all functional – but she did not sleep.

'She is in awe of the world,' Dr Slide said.

'There is much to see of this place,' Jonas said.

'You can take her home. Try singing lullabies to her. Rock her in your arms. Give her a tablespoon of cough syrup. See if that helps. If you see any signs of ill health, bring her back at once.'

The Faccinises took her home. That night, Jonas and Maria sat next to her crib and sang lullabies to her. After the fourth lullaby, Jonas and Maria sang each other to sleep. When Maria woke up the next morning, she heard March singing.

'How can this be?' Maria asked. 'She is a few days old and she can already sing like the Maestro.'

'Soul,' Jonas said.

'It is the song of the sea,' Maria said.

March and Jonas sang along with March.

'She must be hungry,' Jonas said.

'This must be her cry,' Maria said.

March continued to sing with her eyes wide open. She never tired. For three hours, March hummed and sang, not knowing what the words of the song meant.

As soon as the Faccinises' friends heard about the newborn, they came and brought gifts for March.

Their neighbour, Faunna, brought cereal grains. 'Cereal for the cerebral,' she said.

When she walked into the dining room and saw the baby singing, Faunna gasped and coughed at the same time.

'Is this a prank?' Faunna asked.

She looked around the room.

'She can't sleep,' Jonas said. 'But she can sing the tune of the Sirens.'

'She never kicked when she was in my stomach,' Maria said.

Faunna told them that she must go home and bathe the shivers off the back of her neck.

'She is beautiful,' Faunna said.

She rushed out the door. Soon after she left, the Aurianas came over with orange juice and pears.

'Let us see the newborn, so we can celebrate her birth tonight,' Joseph Auriana said.

They brought shiny metallic wind chimes that would hang above her crib. When they heard her sing the song of the sea, they screamed.

'What is wrong with her?' Rona Auriana asked.

'She sings a sad song,' Jonas said.

Rona backed away from March.

'You must take her to the City Council and see what they want to do with such a baby,' Rona said.

'She is too young to sing,' Joseph said. 'She is too young to do anything. She needs to learn how to sleep and start from there.'

Maria picked March up and cradled her child in her arms.

'She has a gift,' she said.

'Who has ever heard of a baby who cannot sleep, but can sing?' Joseph asked. 'This is not right or true.'

'I will have nightmares,' Rona said.

'Something this baby can't have,' Joseph said.

'There's nothing to worry about,' Jonas said. 'She hasn't done anything bad.'

'If you do not take her to the Council, then I will tell them to come here,' Rona said. 'Something must be done. Joseph, we must go.'

Rona's eyes were narrow – her eyebrows were tilted towards the floor. Joseph stared at March with his mouth open. He had stopped breathing, until Rona tugged at his arm and led him out the door. March looked at them and continued to sing in perfect pitch.

'These words are magical,' Jonas said.

Maria turned to Jonas.

'What should we do?' Maria asked. 'They will take her away from us if they think that something is wrong with her.'

'No matter what we try to do, they will find her,' Jonas replied. 'We'll take her to the Council and see what they have to say.'

'She is our daughter,' Maria said.

She picked March up and looked into her eyes. March waved her hands up and down and wiped the tears off her mother's face.

'We will take care of her,' Jonas said. 'But we cannot live in constant fear that the Council will take her away.'

That night, Maria was trying to teach March how to close her eyes. As Jonas walked into their room, he saw Maria on all fours next to March, who was on her back with her arms were stretched out towards Maria's head.

'Like this March,' Maria said.

She put her hands over March's eyes and then moved her hands away. She did it again, but March's eyes were still open. Maria closed her own eyes and opened them repeatedly, but March didn't follow. She sang.

'She already has a stubborn mind,' Jonas said. 'Like yours.'

Jonas and Maria slept on the floor next to March's

crib. March had sung them to sleep with the song of the sea, a sad song of longing and loneliness. She looked around the room, like it was a universe full of stars and comets and moons.

THE FACCINISES TOOK MARCH TO THE COUNCIL. WHEN THEY walked into the meeting room, they saw eleven people sitting around the long rectangular table. The room was filled with cigar smoke. Rinja got up and opened a window to let the smoke out, but the clouds stayed in the room.

'We have come for you to see our baby, March. I am sure you have heard about her unusual abilities through the town's gossip.'

'We've been expecting you,' Rinja said. 'Show us these talents.'

'She cannot sleep,' Maria said. 'You can all see that just by looking at her eyes. They do not close.'

As Maria placed March on the table, the smoke left through the window and the clouds inside the room cleared up. The eleven faces, including Nirana's, looked down at March. Nirana, because of his contribution to the hospital, had been named an honorary member of the Council. He had not heard about March. He stood up from his chair and rubbed his eyes. March was on her back.

'She does nothing,' one Council member said.

'Please put your cigars out,' Nirana said. 'There is a baby in the room.'

The members stubbed their cigars in the ashtray, still keeping their eyes on the baby.

Rinja went up to her and tickled her stomach.

'Sleep,' Rinja said.

March started to sing.

Rinja stepped back. The Council members stopped talking and listened. They bowed their heads, some had tears in their eyes. Nirana mouthed the words March was singing, moving his head from side to side, his hands moving in rhythm to March's song.

'This is unnatural,' Rinja said. 'Why would she do such a thing?'

'This is beautiful,' Nirana said.

'She has done nothing wrong,' Maria said.

The Council members wiped the tears from their faces with handkerchiefs. One of them, Zuben, crouched and looked at March.

'She has done nothing wrong,' he said. 'But how can we trust a baby who can't sleep? How can we trust a week-old baby who can sing the song of the sea?'

'The city will be in unrest,' another Council member said.

Rinja asked the Faccinises to leave the baby with them while they discussed what to do with her. But Jonas and Maria would not let them keep her.

'We just wanted to show you that she is perfectly normal and there is nothing evil about her, that was all,' Jonas said. 'We are not leaving her with you.'

'We understand your love for your baby,' Rinja said. 'Please take her home, but the matter will be discussed. The first signs of any wrongdoing and she will be taken away, if not before, as a precaution.'

'What wrongdoing?' Maria asked. 'She's only a baby.'

Rinja looked straight into Jonas's eyes. March continued to sing. Half the Council members were already asleep.

'She's hungry,' Jonas said.

The Faccinises went back home. The Council members discussed the matter over lunch.

'She must go,' said Zuben. 'I sense that she will bring trouble.'

'The only thing you sense is your hungry stomach,' Nirana said.

The others laughed, then they became serious again. Except for Nirana, they all agreed that the baby must leave. The vote was ten-to-one in favour of exiling March from Kolkaper.

'How can I sleep if there is a baby like that here?' a Council member wanted to know.

'Everyone will stop singing,' another said.

They wanted to take her to the Organization of Scientists to let them figure out what to do with her. There they would perform tests and observe her.

That night, Nirana and Francesca visited the Faccinises, who had just finished eating dinner and were putting March into her crib. They were still hoping she would fall asleep.

'We have cake,' Jonas said by way of greeting.

'Could never say no to cake,' Nirana said. 'My mother would eat all kinds of desserts when she was pregnant with me. I was born with a craving for sugar.'

Nirana turned to Maria and introduced his wife and himself to her. Jonas and Maria realized that this was the couple whose baby had died so soon after she came into the world.

'Our condolences,' Jonas said.

'As quick as a sneeze,' Nirana said.

'May I please see the baby?' Francesca asked.

'We were just trying to put her to bed,' Maria said. 'Let's see what she's up to.'

They walked into the bedroom. March lay in her crib. Her eyes widened when she saw Francesca and she started to sing. Francesca yawned and closed her eyes. Her head drooped. Nirana tapped her on the shoulder, but his head drooped as well. March stopped singing, and the Medallions lifted their heads and opened their eyes.

'A lovely song,' Nirana said.

'She knows what we don't know,' Francesca said. 'Already, at such a young age.'

With tears, Francesca kissed March on top of her head. March stretched her arms out toward her. Francesca picked her up and whispered into her ear. March made a laughing sound and tugged on her ear. Francesca handed her back to Maria.

'She doesn't sleep because the world has too much to offer,' Francesca said. 'She is eager to see what the world has to offer.'

'Let's take her into the living room,' Maria said.

The men stayed behind. Nirana, in a quiet voice, spoke to Jonas, who folded his arms and nodded. He kept looking at the crib as Nirana talked. He started to walk back and forth and then in circles around the crib. After a while, the two men joined Maria and Francesca in the living room.

'We are going to have problems,' Jonas said. 'Monsieur Nirana has important information.'

Francesca and Maria sat down. March lay in her mother's arms.

'The Council has decided to take the baby away,' Nirana said.

'It is not their decision,' Maria said.

'They want to take her to the Organization of Scientists, located near the Cave Forest, and study her.'

'The forest?' Maria asked.

'Cave Forest is for the unusual – it's where people go when they feel shunned.'

'Or because they are shunned,' Jonas said.

'The Organization of Scientists is nearby,' Nirana said. 'If the Organization can't help those who are trying to change themselves so that they fit in with the normal crowd, they are taken to the Forest.'

'What do you think?' Jonas asked.

'I think that they are talented people who are seen as outcasts,' Nirana said.

Maria held March in front of her with her arms stretched out and looked at her eyes.

'Hey you,' she said.

March giggled.

'They come to town sometimes, though they mainly live in the Forest,' Nirana said. 'A whole new world in the Cave. I've talked to them before. Real shy, timid. They are just misunderstood.'

'Can they just take the baby away from us?' Maria asked.

'Legally, no,' Nirana said. 'But the town will scorn this house. It won't be a pleasant life for March. As you know, the Council has strong control over the city. It wouldn't be healthy for the baby to stay here.'

'What do you suggest?' Jonas asked.

'You know about the death of our newborn baby,' Francesca said. 'We know the feeling of a child being taken away, no matter who takes it away. It is arthritis of the soul.'

'We have an alternative to sending March to the Forest,' Nirana said.

He looked at March lying in Maria's arms. Nirana had come up with a plan to send her overseas to Koofay, which was not too far from where Jonas had had to travel for his work with metals. He had friends living there who would look after March until Jonas and Maria could move too.

'You will all be able to live safely,' Nirana said 'As a family.'

He put his hand on Francesca's shoulder.

'It's a beautiful rural area,' Jonas said. 'Filled with ostriches and orange trees. It's at the end of the Bay. I've travelled through it a few times.'

Nirana talked about his Koofay friends, the Armers, whom he had known since his college years.

'They have a daughter and a son, both grown up now and living their own lives. They would love to have a new baby. They would treat her right and teach her to live as a kind person.'

'How much time do you think we have to decide?' Jonas asked.

'Until the end of the week ... about two days,' Nirana said.

'We will make a decision by tomorrow then,' Jonas said.

He looked at Maria. She nodded.

'Thank you for your visit,' Jonas said. 'We appreciate your kindness.'

After they had left, Maria and Jonas discussed what they would do about March.

'She can go to Koofay and live a good life,' Maria said.

'So you do not want her to go to the Cave Forest?' Jonas asked.

'Koofay sounds like a better place,' Maria said. 'And she would have to go through the Scientists first, before going to the Forest. I wonder if we can just take her directly to the Forest and live with her there.'

Jonas told Maria about his conversation with Nirana – about how the Organization of Scientists acts as a filtering system: anyone who goes to the Cave Forest must go through the scientists first, so they know exactly what is going on in the Forest.

'They are constantly observing them,' Jonas said. 'There is never any peace.'

'They are probably too worried that the inhabitants will run amok and take over,' Maria said.

'Are you ready to make the move and leave our lives here?' Jonas asked.

'I'm ready to live on the ocean bed for March,' Maria said. 'And you?'

'I would live on the sun and sweat for the rest of my life for her,' Jonas said.

'Besides,' Maria said. 'If she moves to Koofay, we can definitely be with her. Who knows if we will be able to live with her, or even visit her, if she goes off to the Organization of Scientists.'

'True, just imagine if the Centre gets hold of her. There is nothing wrong with her, but the scientists will insist on running tests on her. It's a pretty scary situation.'

Maria clasped Jonas's hand with her own free hand, the one that wasn't holding March. Their daughter yawned and blinked. They hoped that she would close her eyes and sleep. But she started to sing instead, only not as loud as before. It was quiet – it was a lullaby. Maria had to put her in the crib because the song was making her sleepy. The parents slept peacefully under March's crib with their arms around each other, dreaming of their daughter. When they woke up the next morning, she planned to sing the song of the morning birds to them.

THE FACCINISES WEREN'T ABLE TO DREAM ABOUT THEIR precious March for too long because there was a loud knocking on the door. They didn't hear it at first, but the knocking kept up for several minutes, getting louder all the time. Maria woke up first and shook Jonas. It was early morning and the sun hadn't come up yet.

'Who can that be?'

'Hide March,' Jonas said.

They looked around the room. The knocking was getting louder. Jonas picked March up and hid her in the armoire.

'Please don't sing,' Jonas said.

They went to the door. There were two scientists, both wearing black top hats and matching long lab coats.

'I am Larry.'

He had a thin moustache with its tips curling, pointing towards his glasses, which were black.

'I am Rezna,' said the other man, the one with a goatee and a gold watch that shone under the porch light.

'Scientists,' Maria said.

Larry and Rezna nodded, looked at each other and shook each other's hands.

'How do you do?' Larry said.

'How do you do?' Rezna said.

They turned back to Jonas and Maria and spoke simultaneously: 'Baby.'

'What baby?' Jonas asked.

'The one with the eyes,' Larry said.

'The one with the voice,' Rezna said.

'Not here,' Maria said.

Larry shuffled his hand around in his coat pocket and pulled out a crumpled piece of paper. He held it up to Maria's eyes. 'This paper says there is a baby.'

Rezna pulled out his own piece of paper. 'This paper says we can search your house.'

'A warrant?' Jonas asked.

Larry and Rezna pushed Jonas and Maria aside and walked in. They looked around the foyer and the living room. They checked under the cushions and behind the curtains. They looked at the ceiling. They went to the kitchen and looked in the fridge and in the cabinets. They went to the Faccinises' bedroom. They searched the mattresses and the closets. They went to the four other rooms and searched carefully and then they went to March's room. Jonas held his breath. Maria was trying hard not to look at the armoire. She whispered to Jonas.

'Please don't sing,' she said.

March started to sing. Her voice was muffled, coming from the armoire, but the tune made it through the wooden doors and into their ears. Larry and Rezna stopped moving and looked around the room, trying to figure out where the sound was coming from. Both Maria and Jonas started to sing to drown out March's voice, but the scientists walked towards the armoire and pulled out March.

'Beautiful,' Larry said.

'Stop,' Jonas said.

Rezna held him back. Maria too made a move towards Larry, but with one arm holding March, he held off Maria with the other. Maria, realizing that the baby could get hurt, stopped trying.

'We will take her,' Larry said.

'To the observation room,' Rezna said.

'We will come for her,' Jonas said.

Rezna shrugged. 'Try.'

As the scientists walked out the door, Maria and Jonas started crying. March had stopped singing and she looked into Larry's eyes.

'Cute,' Larry said.

The Faccinises watched the scientists drive away in

their carriage until it was not even a speck in the distance and then they closed the door. Maria sat on the couch, tears streaming down her face.

'I am sorry,' Jonas said.

'It is no one's fault,' Maria said.

'We'll get her back,' Jonas said.

'We'll talk to Nirana to find the whereabouts of the Organization of Scientists,' Maria said. 'We'll get her back.'

'It is so quiet,' Jonas said.

The Faccinises stayed up the rest of the night, waiting for morning to come so they could talk to Nirana.

'This is what March must feel like,' Jonas said.

They held hands and sat in the living room, staring at the door.

Meanwhile, the scientists were travelling back to the observation room. The streets were quiet, except for the sounds of the horse's hooves beating against cobbled roads. The city was still sleeping. Larry held March while Rezna drove. March started to sing and the sound of the hooves was muted by her voice.

'Let's stop and rest and listen,' Rezna said.

Larry nodded.

They sat in the carriage and listened to March sing. Their heads drooped. They yawned. The closed their eyes. Rezna snored. Larry was drooling. March sang. She sang until the morning came and the sun rose and her voice was joined by the surrounding robins. The city was awakening, the roads were gradually coming alive.

Nirana too was out taking a walk when he heard March's voice. He followed it until he saw the carriage.

'Scientists,' Nirana said.

March recognized Nirana and smiled.

'Keep singing,' Nirana said.

There were a few people down the road, making their way towards the carriage. Nirana took March from Larry's arms and cradled her. He casually walked away, whistling and looking at the robins. By the time the people from down the road had arrived, Nirana was safely away and because March had stopped singing, he didn't draw any attention. He went straight to his mansion. There, he told his carriage driver, Mr Thenly, to go to the Faccinises and give them the message that March was in Nirana's care.

Jonas and Maria were still on the couch in the living room. They hadn't slept. They stared at the door fixedly until they heard the knock.

'No more scientists,' Maria said.

Jonas opened the door and Mr Thenly gave them the message.

'I will take you back to Nirana,' Mr Thenly said.

Jonas and Maria didn't change their clothes – they left in their pyjamas, barely remembering to close the door behind them. At the mansion, Maria and Jonas smothered the Medallions with hugs. Maria held March in her arms. The baby wasn't singing, but her wide, round eyes and occasional giggles all spoke of her happiness at being back with her parents.

'She was just singing along with the birds,' Nirana explained. 'And the scientists were fast asleep.'

'Her voice is a lullaby,' Jonas said.

'If she sang loud enough, the whole world would sleep without any trouble,' Maria said.

The Faccinises told the Medallions about their decision and they in turn agreed that it was the right thing to do.

'She will be safe with my friends there,' Nirana said. 'Take the rest of the day and spend time with your daughter. I will travel to Koofay tomorrow to escort March to my friends.'

'But be careful,' Francesca said. 'The scientists will be lurking. They will hunger for her.'

Nirana wrote down the address of their friends' home in Koofay, so the Faccinises could send letters to their daughter.

'The Armers are wonderful people and she will be well looked after there.'

'We will be back soon,' Jonas said.

March moved her arms up and down.

'Cover her in this,' Francesca said.

She gave them a red shawl – it was ragged and full of holes, the threads unravelling.

'No one will suspect anything,' she said.

THE FACCINISES WENT FOR A WALK IN THE PARK. MARIA SPENT
the whole day crying and March sang along, covered in
the red shawl. Despite the looks from other people,
Jonas and Maria let March sing as they looked around
the gardens. People couldn't really tell where the voice
was coming from, nor did they know that March was
just a baby. Jonas and Maria sang along and every now
and then, a small crowd would form around them and
watch them sing. They too clapped and sang along – the
song of the sea was well known throughout Kolkaper.
March stopped singing and Maria and Jonas stopped as
well. The crowds thanked them for the entertainment
and left. Maria picked a rose and showed it to March.

March looked at the red petals. She stuck her arm out
and her fingertips grazed each petal. Maria placed the

rose under March's nose for her to smell. From the park, they went to the market, so she could see the jewellery and fruits. Jonas bought March a silver necklace and a bronze bangle, which she would have to grow into. As evening came, they went back home to pack March's things. The baby remained quiet as she watched her parents shuffle about the room.

'How are you so strong when you know we will be bidding our baby goodbye?' Maria asked.

'Your tears are not a sign of weakness, but firmly rooted in strength,' Jonas replied.

They stayed awake through the night and watched March as she lay in her crib. This was the second night the Faccinises went without sleep, but it didn't bother them one bit. The desire to spend every moment with their baby before she left kept them going. March looked into her parents' eyes, pointed at them and reached for them.

'She wants to see what we see,' Maria said.

'She can see more than we can see,' Jonas said.

'She knows that she is leaving,' Maria said.

Morning came and sunlight streamed in through the kitchen window – an additional source of heat to cook the eggs on the stove.

'Let us take her to the Medallions,' Jonas said.

'Say goodbye to your first home,' Maria said.

March waved her arms around in a circular motion.

The Medallions had just finished breakfast as the Faccinises walked into their house. The smell of syrup and pancakes wafted through the house. Nirana was dressed in a coat and tie. Two small suitcases were in the living room.

'Would you like some pancakes?' Francesca asked.

'Thanks, but we have eggs at home,' Jonas said.

'It is time for us to go now,' Nirana said. 'I would like to reach the harbour before noon.'

Nirana picked up his luggage and opened the door. The carriage and driver were waiting outside. Francesca was staying behind, so she and Nirana kissed and said their goodbyes. She kissed March on the cheek and whispered into her ears.

'You will swim like no other,' Francesca said.

They left for the ocean. By the time they arrived at the harbour, the carriage floor was slippery with Maria's tears.

'Be careful as you step off,' Jonas said.

The sun was approaching its highest point, but the cool ocean winds protected the backs of their necks from its heat. There weren't too many passengers at the harbour for they mostly travelled early in the morning. At that hour, there were mainly fishing boats and seabirds about. There was a wooden shack that served coffee, muffins and liquorice. The homeless were also there, looking out over the ocean. They didn't beg for anything, but sometimes they could be seen bargaining with the seabirds for fish and tyres.

'I have your address and I will write to you as soon as we arrive,' Nirana said.

Maria picked up March, kissed her on the forehead and on each cheek and whispered into her ear.

'Get some sleep,' she said.

Jonas took her from Maria's arms and kissed her on her eyes.

'We will see you again soon,' he said.

He turned to Nirana.

'Please ask the Armers to teach her how to write as soon as possible, so she can write to us,' Jonas said. 'Even if it's only one word.'

Nirana nodded and shook Jonas's hand. He hugged Maria. March and he then boarded the ship; the carriage driver followed them with the luggage.

Maria and Jonas stood there and watched Nirana walk away, but the sun shone right into their faces and, two blinks later, they could no longer see their daughter's eyes. They stood there until the ship left. The carriage driver waited for them, feeding his horses carrots and celery.

'Time to go home,' Jonas said.

'A strange home without our baby,' Maria said.

As the ship went off in one direction, the carriage went off in the other. On their way back, the Faccinises asked the driver to stop at the market, so that they could buy basmati rice and yellow curry. Since it was just after noon, the market was crowded. School was done for the summer and children were running around while their parents were looking for vegetables and lamps. The children used fruits as footballs and baseballs – splotches of yellows and oranges and greens and reds were flying through the air. The market workers yelled at them, but the children continued to have fun. Maria and Jonas bought their rice and curry and walked back to their carriage. On the way, Jonas bumped into a younger man with no hair and a gold tooth.

'Pardon,' Jonas said, moving aside.

'I am going to kill you,' the bald-headed man said.

Jonas and Maria didn't reply. Maria looked back and saw that the man was following them. The carriage was still at a distance.

'Stop,' the gold-tooth man shouted. 'You are the parents of the odd baby. I heard about you two.'

Jonas turned around and faced the man. He told Maria to keep walking towards the carriage, but she stayed with Jonas. She had to constantly move her body to release the tension within – she could feel the pressure of her blood beating against the inside of her skin.

Jonas stood still. His eyebrows were tense and his mouth slightly open, showing his teeth grinding against each other.

'Stop following us,' Jonas said.

The bald-headed man held an avocado in one hand and a knife in the other.

'You cannot live here and bring such witchery to our town,' he said. 'I have heard of your baby. All three of you must go.'

The sweat on his bald head dripped down his face and neck. His red eyes matched the burnt skin on his head and cheeks.

'We have done nothing to harm you or this town,' Jonas said. 'And she is gone.'

'My daughter had just died of pneumonia,' he shouted.

'Our condolences,' Maria said.

'She died the same day your daughter was born,' the man continued. 'I know, because my daughter was in the next room.'

He started to pace back and forth and in circles.

'I heard what the doctor said about the singing newborn,' he said. 'My daughter is dead because of the birth of your daughter.'

'That isn't possible,' Jonas replied. 'I am sorry to hear of your daughter's death, but neither we, nor our baby, had anything to do with it.'

Jonas's voice was calm and firm. He held his hands close to his sides to block the man in case he attacked them. Maria was standing not too far behind. The carriage driver saw that the Faccinises were in trouble and headed towards them. Just as the carriage pulled up, the man with the gold tooth lunged forward with his knife. Jonas moved out of the way, but not quickly enough, and the knife sliced the side of his body. He fell to his knees, grabbing his side. Maria ran towards her husband, but the man stood in her way.

'This is vengeance for my daughter,' he said.

He stepped towards her and stabbed her just above the stomach. With a gasp, she looked into her assailant's eyes and fell to the ground. Maria whispered to her husband that she was going to sleep. Jonas looked at

Maria and then at the man with the gold tooth. The man's knife was already in motion to stab him, but a bullet stopped him, causing him to fall backwards. As the man died, he murmured his last word, 'Flora.' Jonas looked behind him and saw the driver with a gun pointed toward the bald man. The smell of gunpowder and blood mixed together as Jonas lifted Maria's head. The driver helped Jonas to his feet.

'Help me pick her up,' the driver said. 'We must go to the hospital right away.'

Jonas couldn't speak. He helped the driver lift Maria into the carriage.

The driver helped Jonas into the carriage and told him to lie on his unwounded side. Then he ripped off the sleeve of his own shirt and wrapped it tight around Jonas's body.

'The blood must stop,' he said.

The driver went back to the bald man who lay dead on the ground. He dragged the man to the carriage and placed him in the back compartment.

'Enemy or no enemy, he should be treated as any other human.'

The driver then drove to the hospital. Jonas lay on his side and Maria lay before him on the opposite side. He looked at her and sang in gasps, sounding like a broken flute. He looked to his left and saw the dead man with the knife still firmly held in his hand. Two avocadoes fell out of his pocket, rolling around on the carriage seat. The knife was the last thing Jonas saw before he lost consciousness. The driver reached the hospital and sought help from nurses and doctors who were just finishing their lunch. Dr Slide went to the carriage with a napkin stained with mustard tucked into his shirt. One of the nurses was still chewing her broccoli as she reached the carriage to help the wounded into the hospital. Once they were in the hospital, the driver left for the Medallion mansion to inform Francesca of the situation.

Maria was kept in the same room where her stabber's daughter had passed away and Jonas was in the room in which March had been born. The doctor had declared that the bald man was dead.

'His vitals are all unimportant,' Dr Slide said.

Maria was barely breathing. Dr Slide and his partner, Dr Hingen, tended to her wound. Blood dripped to the floor as the doctors tried to feel for any wounded organs. The stab was too deep to tell. They assumed that her lungs were pierced, maybe even her heart. Down the hall, two nurses were taking care of Jonas. They were stitching his wound with threads that had been imported from overseas. The two doctors knew that the only thing they could do was to clean and sew Maria's stab wound.

'We need to invest in some technology,' Dr Slide said. 'I have heard of robots and machines.'

'Our future is their past,' Dr Hingen said.

Maria convulsed in spasms. As soon as her wound was shut, the doctors gave her a shot that would calm the nerves in her spine. Her heart started to pulsate in a regular pattern.

'She is between life and death,' Dr Slide said. 'We have no control over which way she goes.'

Jonas regained consciousness. The nurses had just finished stitching his side. Remembering what had happened, he asked about his wife. The nurses told him of her critical condition, and that he must rest and drink water.

'I have just finished resting,' Jonas said. 'Let me see my wife.'

He got up, limped down the hallway and looked though every door for Maria. He saw the killer lying dead in one room, and in the next room he saw Maria.

'Wake up Maria,' he told her.

She opened her eyes and looked at Jonas's chin. He held her hand.

'You have blood on your chin,' she whispered.

'Can you breathe?' he asked.

'I am living off someone else's breath,' Maria said. 'It cannot be mine, my lungs are dead. I can feel them limp inside my body.'

'Rest,' Jonas said. 'No more talking.'

'There is couscous in the kitchen,' Maria said.

Francesca walked into the room with the driver. She knelt down next to Maria's bed and bowed her head. She looked at Maria, whose eyes were closed. Francesca took her hand and looked at her body, now held together with stitches.

'She is breathing someone else's air,' she said.

Jonas nodded. Francesca kept a plate of rose petals on the bedside table. Jonas breathed in its scent.

'A rose for a rose,' he said.

Maria didn't open her eyes for the rest of the night, but continued to breathe using someone else's lungs. Jonas stayed in her room all night. Francesca went home to bring back food for Jonas. Before she left, Jonas thanked the driver.

'I never got a chance to thank you,' Jonas said. 'If it weren't for you, we would have been dead.'

'I acted on instinct,' he said. 'I'm not a fighter. The Medallions show great care for you two, and I was just doing what they would have wanted me to do.' He sighed and shook his head. 'If only I had come earlier, none of this would have happened. I apologize.'

'None of us were expecting such an event,' Jonas said. 'I apologize for involving you in this horrible event. I do not even know the name of the man who saved my life.'

'Mr Thenly,' the driver replied.

'Thank you, Mr Thenly.'

The driver nodded and walked out of the room. Francesca told Jonas that she would be back with food and followed Mr Thenly out of the room. Jonas sat by Maria's bedside and stayed up through the night. He thought about March and how she had the energy to stay awake every night. He looked at the ceiling light.

'You are remarkable,' Jonas said. 'I hope one day your mother will be able to wake up and see your eyes again. I will try my best to be like you.'

The next morning, Francesca brought vegetables and rice and then went back home. She had to take care of her husband's errands while he was away.

'My thoughts are crumbs,' Francesca said. 'But I will be back to share them with you and Maria.'

The doctors would walk in and out of Maria's room to check on her condition, which stayed the same through the night. Jonas, the pain in his side decreasing, would talk to Maria in the hope that she might hear his voice and wake up. He asked her if she thought that Nirana and March had reached Koofay.

'It will be quite a journey,' he said.

ON THE SHIP, NIRANA AND MARCH SAT AT THE FRONT END OF the vessel, which was designated for the wealthier travellers. The wind was fair and the ocean was calm, allowing the ship to sail smoothly across the waters. Nirana laughed as he saw the bewildered baby trying to figure out why the ground was moving. She pointed to the window.

'The sky', Nirana said.

She pointed at the sun.

'Light', Nirana said.

Nirana sang love songs to her – the only type of songs he knew – and March sang along.

'I would sing these songs to Francesca,' Nirana said. 'Every morning and every night.' He looked out and saw a seagull flying in circles. 'Since we were five years old.'

He picked her up and rocked her in his arms, following the motion of the ship. He noticed that her diaper needed changing.

Realizing that he had never changed a baby before, he thought for a few seconds about the process involved. He looked through one of the small suitcases for the diapers and baby clothes that Maria had packed. He picked up a diaper and studied it carefully to see how the attachments worked. He took the cloth off March, and then the stained diaper and asked one of the clerks to throw them away. The clerk grimaced, placed them in a small trashcan and took the bin away.

As he was leaving, Nirana asked him, 'Kind sir, would you know how to put one of these on a baby?'

The clerk replied, 'I can travel across an ocean without a compass and find my destination in the darkest of nights. I do not know how to change a baby's diaper.'

His frown turned into a small smile as he left the cabin. Nirana looked at the diaper and then at March. He pulled out some safety pins from the bag and began to attach the diaper to the baby. He figured out the process eventually. March wiggled her legs and playfully tugged at Nirana's fingers as he was putting the finishing touches on her diaper. He laughed.

'If Francesca could have seen me now,' he said. 'I hope she is doing okay. I hope the Faccinises will be okay without you.'

March lifted her arms and burped.

'Lovely,' Nirana said.

March sang Nirana to sleep and while he was sleeping, she looked out the cabin window and watched the seabirds soar in circles and in patterns. She pointed at them and looked at Nirana. She kept pointing at them until Nirana woke up.

'Yes,' Nirana said. 'Lovely.'

He fell into a daze as he watched the seabirds fly and when March started to sing again, his head began drooping.

'This has been one sleepy trip.' He looked at March. 'At least for me.'

There was a knock on the cabin door. It was one of the captains.

'I am Captain Don,' he said. 'And is the singing coming from this cabin?'

March was quiet. Nirana nodded his head.

'It was me,' I said. 'I was trying to sing this baby to sleep.'

'You have sung the ship to sleep,' Captain Don said. 'We even travelled off course for a bit.'

Nirana looked at March and shook his head, smiling.

'It is such a lovely song,' Captain Don said. 'Everyone on board fell asleep, including myself and Captain Neptune.'

Nirana apologized.

'I hope that it won't happen again,' he said.

'I understand the need for singing,' Captain Don said. 'Especially while at sea.' He looked at March and added, 'And with a baby. But please refrain from doing so for the rest of the voyage.'

'Absolutely,' Nirana said. 'I will try my best.'

'I even saw a dolphin on its back,' Captain Don said. 'Sleeping.'

He gestured toward the cabin window. 'Hear that?' the captain asked. 'Those are snoring sharks.'

Nirana shook the captain's hand and apologized again. The captain commented on the beauty of the baby.

'Hopefully,' Captain Don said, 'she'll follow suit and sleep as well.' He walked out of the cabin, calling out a 'back to my duties' to them.

After he had left, Nirana picked March up and kissed her on the forehead.

'March,' he said. 'The baby who sang the sea to sleep.'

MARIA WAS STILL IN CRITICAL CONDITION.

'It has been six days since she stirred,' Dr Slide said.

'I have counted every second,' Jonas replied.

'How many?' Dr Slide asked.

'518,400 seconds,' Jonas replied. '401. 402. 403. 404. 405. 406.'

'Keep counting,' Dr Slide said.

Jonas had been living in the hospital for the past six days, barely leaving Maria's side. Francesca would bring him food every morning and mid-evening. Jonas hadn't bathed for the past week and the room was beginning to smell of his curry and sweat. The evening of the sixth day, Francesca visited Jonas to give him some company.

'Nirana and March will arrive in Koofay soon enough,' she said.

'I hope all is well,' he replied.

'There is a rumour going around that the sea would fall asleep from time to time while they were travelling,' Francesca said.

'Do you have a telephone in your house?' Jonas asked.

'We bought one about a year ago. Odd things. They run on a magic of some sort.'

'I've heard about them,' Jonas said. 'If you don't mind, and I would pay of course, would there be a way to call them?'

'Of course,' Francesca said. 'And don't worry about paying. This will be a perfect use of the telephone.'

The Medallions were the only ones in Kolkaper to have a telephone. They realized that this limited its use.

'Whom can we call?' Francesca would ask.

'Let's go for a walk,' Nirana would reply.

Francesca looked at Jonas. She breathed in and coughed.

'If you like,' Francesca said, 'I could stay here and you can go back home and clean yourself.'

'I know I smell,' he replied. 'But I'm afraid that I cannot leave this room.'

Jonas ran his hand through his hair. Loose strands fell out.

'I almost lost my job because of my long leave of absence,' he said. 'A colleague of mine came in earlier today to inform me.'

'These are troubled times,' Francesca said, 'Days full of fallen pine cones.'

'Truthfully,' Jonas confessed, 'I had completely forgotten about the Science and Metal Lab. However, an hour later, realizing the situation I am in, my superior actually visited me here and gave me my job back.'

'That is good news,' Francesca replied. 'I will go now and tend to the house. Perhaps Nirana will call on the telephone soon enough.'

'Thank you for the food and sorry about the smell. If I can give you some coins, could you please bring me some aloe leaves?'

'Don't worry about the coins, I have a garden full of soap.'

Jonas thanked her and sat down again in the chair beside Maria.

'Please wake up,' he said.

He put his head on the side of her bed. After a week of restless nights, he was finally able to sleep for a bit. He dreamt about fried eggs, bathtubs and metals. He dreamt about March and Maria holding her at a fountain made of stone. But some small movements from Maria woke him up. The bed sheets moved a bit where her knees were. Jonas looked up from Maria's legs to her face. Her eyes opened, she lifted her head.

'Please bathe,' she said. 'You are creating a whole new world of demons with the stench of your body.'

She closed her eyes and her head fell back onto the pillow. Jonas left the hospital room and bathed outside using a fire hydrant. When he returned, he saw Francesca sitting in the room with a bowl of lentils and rice.

'You look refreshed,' she said.

'I feel much better, like a snake that has just shed its old skin.'

She handed the bowl of rice and lentils to Jonas. He took his time eating the food. Although he was hungry, Jonas was always patient, never eating too fast or too slow.

'One day I will cook for you,' Jonas said. 'I am a good cook. I can make big bowls of cereals.'

'I have good news,' Francesca said. 'Early this morning, I received a telephone-ring from Nirana. They have arrived safely and the Armers were there to receive them.'

'I miss her,' Jonas said.

'Everyone is doing okay. Apart from a few adventures Nirana had in changing March's diapers, everything is well.'

Francesca and Jonas looked at Maria.

'I informed Nirana about the events of the past week,' Francesca continued. 'He sends his condolences and wishes the best for everyone.'

'Wish him a safe trip back,' Jonas said.

'March began to cry in the background, so Nirana had to leave,' Francesca said. 'He will use the telephone again and you can come over anytime and use ours.'

'It's like March knew something bad had happened,' Jonas said.

Jonas looked at Maria and bowed his head. Then he looked at the walls and then at Francesca. He clasped his hands. He unclasped his hands and put his fingertips together. He scratched his knees and looked at the ceiling lights.

'The humming sounds like flies,' Jonas said.

'A constant reminder,' Francesca said.

'March will find her way,' Jonas said. 'She will sing herself through life. She will keep her eyes open until she has seen all that needs to be seen.'

Francesca went up to Maria and fixed her blanket.

'What will happen to us?' Jonas asked.

Francesca rubbed Maria's forehead and wrists.

'What will happen to Maria? If she is gone, I will be no one.'

'She will find her way,' Francesca said. 'Whether it's in this life or another life, that we cannot say.'

IN KOOFAY, THE ARMERS WELCOMED MARCH AND NIRANA into their house.

'A wonderful baby,' Sofi said. 'Amazing how she can sing like that. I couldn't even talk with such skill when I was in my teens.'

'She will be safe here,' Ons said. 'Please stay as long as you like.'

'Just for a day or two,' Nirana replied. 'I have much work to do in Kolkaper. The Faccinises wished they could come, but they have much to tend to at home.'

'Take your time,' Ons said. 'Sofi and I have cooked dinner for tonight. For dessert, we will have pudding, lemon pudding.'

'Delicious,' Nirana replied. 'Please excuse me, I must refresh my face. May I use the telephone afterwards?'

'Use it as much as you like,' Sofi said. 'So far we've used it only four times.'

He went to the bathroom. Ons and Sofi played with March.

'It has been such a long time since we held a baby,' Sofi said. 'I miss those days.'

'I do too,' Ons replied. 'But it is all a process, isn't it – the process of life.'

March was looking back and forth between Sofi and Ons. She put her fingers out to touch Ons's face and felt the smooth texture of his chin.

'She seems mature for her age,' Ons said.

'That she is,' Sofi said. 'As if she has been alive for a hundred years.'

March started to sing. Stretching out her hands, she touched everything in sight. The multi-coloured cushioned furniture attracted her attention the most.

'Unbelievable,' Sofi and Ons said at the same time.

Their heads drooped. Suddenly March began to cry. Nirana rushed into the room with a heavy brow. His eyes were watery. He sat down on the sofa and consoled the baby and then looked at the Armers. Nirana told the Armers about the Faccinises and the stabbing incident.

'How are they now?' Sofi asked.

'Maria has been unconscious since and has been at the hospital,' Nirana said. 'Jonas's injury is in the process of healing and he is alive and well.'

He looked at March.

'He sleeps at the hospital, in Maria's room.'

Nirana picked up March and rocked her gently from side to side.

'You would have been a great father,' Ons said. 'Our condolences to the Faccinises. We wish well for them.'

'Come,' Sofi said. 'Let us eat now. You two must be famished after the boat ride.'

They went into the dining room which was lit by a sparkling chandelier, a three-levelled creation made of glass and diamonds. March was in a crib that had been used for the Armers' children when they were babies. Yellow curry and vegetables decorated the table – celery, carrots, peas and corn.

'I didn't realize how hungry I was until just now, seeing this food,' Nirana said.

'We have plenty,' Ons replied. 'Will March eat?'

'Not until tonight, when we are sleeping. Then she will be hungry.'

Nirana stayed with the Armers for one day. He spent as much time as possible with March. They went for walks in the park and to the beach to watch the waves and the seabirds. March sang, and the seabirds started to slow down; some fell into the ocean. People gathered around, listening with excitement and watching the seabirds fall asleep. There, in Koofay, they weren't worried about the baby who could sing.

'You're special,' Nirana said.

He held her up to the sun and the sunlight framing the baby made her look like a glowing spectacle – a being somewhere between a human and a wonder.

March's mouth was wide open, making odd shapes as she sang the high and low notes of the song.

The night before Nirana left, he held March in his arms and looked into her eyes. March looked into his eyes too and raised her arm to trace his face with her fingers. She opened her mouth like she wanted to say something, but nothing came out. Nirana didn't say anything either and kissed her on the forehead.

'Take care of the Armers,' he said. 'They're sweet people. They will guide you as you will guide them.'

THE ARMERS SOON REALIZED THAT MARCH WAS AN EASY BABY to care for, easier than their own children had been. The first years of her life went by quickly for all of them. Jonas called as often as he could and spoke to the Armers and he would ask them to put March next to the telephone so he could hear her murmur and babble. 'She sounds eloquent,' Jonas would tell the Armers. Calling the Armers was the one bright spot in Jonas's life as the coma reigned over Maria.

The Armers taught March how to read and write by the age of five, which was two years after she had learned how to use the bathroom on her own. 'This is easier than trying to sleep,' March would say. She had yet to close her eyes at night – those hours when the world was at rest, she would learn as much as possible about math and science and literature. She would do jumping jacks, hoping that she would eventually tire herself out, but after jumping for two days straight, she realized that it wouldn't work.

When she was ten, Sofi gave her a canvas and three tubes of paint. She would wear an apron and stand outside on the porch, painting splotches of blues, reds and yellows. Ons would stand outside with her, smoking his pipe and telling her to mix the various colours. He did not know how to paint, but he acted like he did.

'Great texture,' he would say.

As she grew older, in addition to painting, her favourite activities included singing and playing football. She was the leading scorer for her team, averaging two goals a game. She could have scored more, but she made sure to keep the team involved. Every Saturday, she would spend one hour listening to the Armers' record player and then after, she would try to emulate the voices of Pavarotti, Kiri Te Kanawa, Buddy Holly and Gilbert and Sullivan. Sofi taught her how to play the violin when she was eleven. March would become frustrated because she had trouble matching the fingers with the strings. From late at night till early morning, she would practice until she came close to perfection. Sometimes, when she wanted to throw the instrument out the window, the birdsong from outside helped her keep her patience. She learnt more from the birds outside on the branches of the nearby trees than from Sofi. March wouldn't tell her this though, because she knew that Sofi took pride in teaching her the violin.

March formed a passion for the body and was curious about how bodily processes worked. When she was twelve years old, she was injured in a friendly game of football. She scraped her knee on the dirt. Instead of crying and asking for help, March sat there gazing into the open cut. Another student ended up crying and running home after seeing March's torn skin. March limped back home and showed Ons and Sofi the cut. They put formaldehyde on the wound to keep it from getting infected. March was fascinated by the reaction of the blood with alcohol and laughed on hearing the sizzle. She asked Sofi to put more, but Sofi laughed and said, 'Any more and you will spit formaldehyde from your mouth.' From then on, March would purposefully get cuts and bruises to see all the various kinds of scrapes and healing. She loved scabs.

'I want to be a doctor,' she said.

She was a curious teenager – always asking questions and always wondering why. Ons and Sofi were glad to answer her questions to the best of their ability. For the most part, they had no problems with her inquiries, but when she asked the Armers in the kitchen how giraffes were born, they were stumped. They did not have that problem with their own children, because they had learnt about reproduction at a later age, in school.

'The teacher will tell you about that,' Sofi said. 'Be patient.'

But March wanted to know as soon as possible. She would walk about the market, asking everyone she knew about how giraffes were born. Most of the responses were either surprised looks or laughs and then they would walk away without answering her question. She finally found out from one of the orange sellers, Mario. He told her while selling oranges to customers. Some were angered and others were embarrassed by their conversation. He lost business that day, but made a good friend. March stood and listened to Mario intently. She accepted everything he said, showing no emotion. After Mario finished explaining the birth of a giraffe, March stood there for a few seconds without saying anything. Mario continued to sell his oranges to the few customers who didn't care about their conversation.

'Really?' March said.

Mario nodded his head.

'And what about humans?'

'It's a little different,' Mario replied.

'How so?'

Mario explained. March listened, again, her face expressionless.

'Are you sure?' she asked.

'Yes, it fits perfectly, like the ocean and the sky. That will be forty-five.'

The customer handed over some coins and rushed off.

'Yes, I have seen it before,' Mario said. 'I helped my mother give birth three years ago, when I was eleven. There was liquid called placenta everywhere. It looked like the gel that Mr Jojere wears in his hair.'

Mario pointed across the street, where Mr Jojere was standing. He was gelling his hair and slicking it back and then, as they watched, he moved on to his moustache. Some of the gel fell on the ground.

'Thank you kindly,' Mario said.

When there were no customers, Mario drew diagrams on pieces of paper towels to help March understand.

'So how long does the baby stay in the stomach?'

'Roughly one to nine months. The mother's stomach becomes as big as one of those hot-air balloons. The ones you see at the circus.'

'Do you have any children?' March asked.

'No, I do not,' Mario replied. 'But I have dreamt about it.'

March thanked Mario for his time, bought a few oranges and went back home. She told Sofi and Ons that she had learnt about creating babies from a friend.

'And what do you think?' Ons asked.

Both Ons and Sofi looked at March, waiting for a response.

'Funny,' she said.

'Who told you?' Ons asked.

'Mario,' March said. 'He calls reproduction "winter".'

'Mario, as in Mario the orange-seller?' Sofi asked.

March nodded.

'He is a gentle young man and a very good orange-seller,' Sofi said.

'He is a kind boy,' Ons said. 'But why call it winter?'

'Because,' March explained, 'he said in his dreams, he was born in snow.'

'That's odd,' Sofi said. 'It never snows here.'

'Maybe in his dreams, he is in another land, like Kolkaper.'

Ons and Sofi were silent for a few seconds. They had never heard March mention Kolkaper before. They looked at each other and then Ons turned to March.

'How do you know about Kolkaper?' Ons asked.

'We learnt about it at school,' March said. 'Ms Thibidia was talking about metals and she mentioned that Kolkaper is one of the leading cities for the study of metals and alchemy.'

March bade them goodnight and went to her room. She didn't sleep. She couldn't sleep, but she thought about giraffes.

AS MARCH THOUGHT ABOUT GIRAFFES IN KOOFAY, JONAS WAS
pouring water into a cup from a pitcher in his kitchen in
Kolkaper. He walked into the room where Maria lay.
She had been moved into the house from the hospital;
it had now been twelve years since the knifing. The
Faccinises had not been able to visit March in Koofay.
Jonas could barely work because of his wife's condition.
When he did attend the Lab, Francesca would stay over
to look after Maria.

Eventually, Jonas forgot about his job and stopped
going to the lab, as his mind was too consumed by
thoughts of Maria. For the first few years after March's
departure, he had kept up his contact with the Armers
and his daughter through telephone and letters carried
by ships. But gradually, his depression had led him to

tune out the rest of the world. Only the Medallions kept in touch with the Armers. Only the Medallions kept in touch with the Faccinises. Francesca and Nirana became the unofficial parents of Jonas and Maria. The Medallions would talk about their future, like the two were their children.

'When will March know about her true parents?' Francesca asked.

'That is uncertain,' Nirana replied. 'It has been so many years and March lives her own life now. Poor Jonas doesn't even know where he is anymore. His room is his world and Maria is his life.'

'Since that stabbing,' Francesca said, 'they have lived in an uneven universe.'

'Fortune's fools,' Nirana replied.

Francesca's grey hair matched the greyness of her husband's moustache, the only hair he had left. The wrinkles on Nirana's forehead sagged, causing his eyebrows to droop. Francesca's arthritis forced her to walk in a bent shape. When she walked up the stairs in her house, she would bend forward with a cane in one hand and look down on each step to maintain her balance. When she walked down the stairs, she would bend backward with a cane in hand and look at the ceiling to remain stable.

'I now have a different view of the earth,' Francesca would say to her friends.

'I woke up one morning and saw an old man in the mirror,' Nirana would say to his friends.

Nirana had retired from his legal profession. He and his wife moved out of their mansion and bought a house next to the Faccinises. The Medallions were the only people Jonas found himself talking to, but his forgetfulness had caused problems there too. They visited him almost every day and each time they had to identify themselves to him afresh. He only knew one person – Maria – and she barely showed any signs of life. Her heart would beat once every thirty seconds. Every now and then, in the middle of the night, Maria would awaken from her sickness and tell Jonas to stop his snoring.

'Your snore will cause a great earthquake,' she would tell him and then fall back into her coma.

Jonas, through stress and an unhealthy life, became old too soon. His bent back and stiff joints added to his age. His forgetfulness gave him no end of trouble, not least when he couldn't find his glasses. His wife, however, did not age. The doctor gave her nutrition shots and they taught Jonas how to do this so that he could do it at home. It was the only task Jonas would not forget. All else were lost memories.

MARCH BECAME A LADY. SHE FINISHED HER COLLEGE YEARS IN Koofay. She studied biology and medicine. She wanted to become one of the best doctors in the area.

'Makes sense,' Ons said.

'The life she does not know has led her to this field,' Sofi said.

Her legs had tightly packed calves and her lungs were strong as they had been worked from the day she was born. The combination of her parents' skin colour and the Koofay sun gave her a coffee-and-cream complexion. Her black hair, which matched the colour of her eyes, went down to her shoulders. Her eyes had yet to close – they were constantly looking around, studying and observing.

When she was twenty-one, Ons and Sofi both passed

away on the same day. They died in bed. Ons was
snoring and Sofi slept quietly. A sudden loud gasp of
breath capped by a loud snort marked Ons's last breath.
Sofi woke up in fright and the shock to her system
caused her death. Neither of them knew that the other
had died, though they were right next to each other.

March found them in bed the next morning. She
shook them to wake them up, then checked their pulses
and realized that they were gone. She called the hospital
and the funeral home right after. The service was held
three days later at a nearby church. A small number of
people attended. Though the Armers had many friends,
most of them had already passed away. Their biological
children, Fey and Fife, came from overseas to attend the
service. The last time March had met them, she had
been only a few years old.

'They were beautiful people,' March said.

'They were extraordinary,' Fey said. 'I wish we had
been home more often, but our lives kept us overseas.'

None of them cried at the service.

'My, you have grown into a beautiful young lady,' Fife
said. 'The last time I saw you, the top of your head
tickled my knees.'

'I owe it to my parents,' March said. 'Through their
guidance and love, I've become true.'

Fey and Fife looked at each other for a second and
then nodded. They wanted to tell her about her
background and her true parents. But they didn't know
whether it was right or wrong to give her such

information, so they kept silent and watched the Armers being taken out from the crematorium to the graveyard. They were to be cremated, but neither their skin nor their bones would burn.

'These bodies will not burn,' the cremator said. 'It must be something in their skin. They must be buried.'

At the graveyard, the undertaker dug the earth for two hours until the land was ready for the Armers.

'Their bones will enrich the soil,' the undertaker said.

He pointed to a little patch just next to the grave, where there were daffodils.

'These have just sprouted,' he said.

On the last day of their stay, the siblings asked March about her relationship with their parents. They were in the kitchen of the Armers' house, sipping tea and eating scones.

'It was a close relationship,' March said. 'They taught me everything. They disciplined me when I needed to be and they loved me as well.'

She looked at her teacup and ran her fingers along its rim.

'I wish I could have done more for them,' she said. 'I had dreams of buying them a nice house near the Koofay harbour, where they could see the ocean talking to the banks of this land.'

'They would have loved that,' Fey said. 'Especially Father.'

'What do you plan on doing in the future?' Fife asked.

'I will have to see when the future comes,' March said.

She knew she wanted to be in love and she knew she would want to have a child.

'Right now, I will be a doctor-in-training,' March said.

Fey made some more tea. Fife took some more scones out of the oven.

'I've never been to the circus,' March said. 'I would also like to see the circus some day.'

'I think they will come again during the spring,' Fey said.

They spent the rest of the night talking about their childhood and their work. Fife explained to March what her job in Switzerland as a ballroom dancing teacher was like.

'It's wonderful,' Fife said. 'All I have to do is dance around the room until I become dizzy.'

Fey lived in Hawaii.

'You should see the volcanoes erupting,' he said. 'It is just like the circus. The birth of lava is a spectacle. It's sparkling rain, furious and hot.'

'I must see this some day,' March replied. 'I have yet to leave Koofay. But now that school is finished, I will travel and see the world.'

Fey and Fife went to bed early that night because they had to be at the harbour early in the morning. March sat in her room and thought about the world and what she wanted to do with her life.

While the siblings slept, March left the house and

visited Mario at the café. He still sold oranges in the market, but at night, he also sold pastries and coffee at the Espresso Expresso café. The place wasn't busy because there was a musical event at the Auditorium that night. Three tenors from Africa were on tour and the town had gone to the Auditorium to hear them sing. Mario was standing behind the counter, staring through the window, watching people walk by. He saw March walk in and tried to look busy. He pulled out a rag from his pocket and wiped the counters. He had cleaned them about a half-hour ago, but he didn't want to look lazy on the job, especially in front of March.

'If you clean the counter any more,' March said. 'It will begin to float.'

'What are you doing tonight?' Mario asked.

'I came to bother you.'

'Not at all,' Mario said.

'Do you plan on living here your whole life?' March asked.

'My condolences,' he replied. 'I heard about your parents and I never got a chance to see you after they passed away.'

'Thank you. But do you think you are going to leave Koofay?'

'Would you like anything to drink?' he asked.

He revved up the espresso machine.

'It's not like it will keep me up all night,' March said.

They stared at the machine as it rattled for twenty seconds. Mario poured her a drink and then one for himself.

'So what were you asking?' Mario said.

March repeated the question. Mario looked out the window and told her he had never thought about it before.

'All I know is oranges and coffee and that is all I need to know. I am happy with my life,' Mario said.

'If I leave, would you want to move with me?' she asked. 'I love this place and the people here, but I am curious about the world and what there is to find out there.'

'I have no ties here,' Mario replied. 'My family have all died, bless their dead eyes, and I am the only remaining Baracha.'

'We are mirrors,' March replied. 'Give me some time, I have to clean the house of my parents' belongings, and then we can leave.'

'No rush,' Mario told her.

They finished their espresso and talked about the three tenors who were in town.

'They're from Africa,' Mario said. 'I saw one of the singers here last night. He said he was two centuries old. He only looked about seventy or eighty.'

'How so?' March asked.

'He told me that the sweetness of music keeps him young.'

'Are they still singing?' March asked.

Mario nodded and told her they would be singing through the night. 'They stop when the sun comes up, because that is when the morning birds begin to sing their own songs.'

March asked Mario if he would like to go, but he declined, saying that he must work until morning.

'If the boss catches me leaving work again,' Mario said, 'he will kill my cat.'

March left for the Auditorium, which was a few blocks away. When she arrived, there was a crowd of people standing outside, drinking coffee and smoking cigars. March walked through the crowd and through the door of the Auditorium. She could faintly hear the voices of the tenors though the walls. An usher opened the door and let her in.

'This music is not for the ears, but for the soul,' he said.

As the doors opened, the sound of three voices filled the air. She looked at the seated audience – their heads faced the ground and their eyes were closed, as if they were praying. She looked at the three singers on stage. Chandeliers and lamps on posts lit the room. When she asked the usher why the room was so bright, he replied that the lights were actually dim, but as the tenors sang, their voices caused the lights to burn brighter. The usher showed her to an empty seat in the last row and went back to the door.

Their voices travelled from the stage and straight into her body. She could barely move or blink her eyes. As they kept singing, she felt her head wanting to droop and her eyes wanting to close, as if they were under some kind of magic spell. She understood why the others had their faces down. 'Like the sirens,' she whispered. March resisted the temptation of the voices' magic and forced herself to look at the singers. They were standing, dressed in black tuxedos with shirts that had ruffled collars. They were slim and old-looking, but their eyes were strong and vibrant. She wondered which one was the 200-year-old man, and figured it was the one standing on the right with a marble cane in his hand. She sat there for hours. The performance went on till the early morning, which was about when the audience awoke from their trance and left with mournful looks on their faces.

'One of the worst performances ever,' one man said as he walked out the door, rubbing his eyes.

Another old lady said that she would never listen to music again after such a bad performance. March couldn't understand – she thought everyone was enjoying the performance. She looked behind her and saw the usher still standing at the door. He was the only other one who had not fallen under the tenors' magic. March got up and walked to the usher.

'Why are they mad with the performance?'

'They all fell asleep.'

'What about the lights?' March asked. 'And I felt like putting my head down and closing my eyes, but not out of boredom, but as if I was under some kind of spell.'

The usher opened the door to let out a few more people with scowling faces.

'The aura from their voices did cause the chandeliers to brighten,' he said. 'But only because this room recognizes the beauty of their singing. The people, on the other hand, were listening to the music with only their ears and they became bored.'

'And you?' March asked.

'I recognized it even without hearing them sing. As soon as they walked in, I felt the blood in my veins and arteries flow with clarity and ease. And the same happened to you. You are a beautiful person, inside and out, and the voices stuck to you like earth to the sun.'

'Is it true that one of them is 200 years old?' March asked.

'His name is Blue – he is the one standing on the right with the cane.' The usher pointed towards him. 'But don't let him fool you. He uses the cane not because of his age, but because of a fishing accident.'

'What happened?'

'He accidentally caught a shark.'

The two stood at the doorway and watched people leave. The sun was beginning to rise and the birds began to sing their own songs. The tenors stopped singing. They bowed their heads and began to walk down the steps of the stage.

As they walked out, Blue looked at March.

'Listen to the birds,' he said. 'They sing a sad song.'

March looked into the tenor's strong, vibrant blue eyes. He walked past her but after a few steps, stopped and turned around.

'Your eyes,' Blue said. 'They sing the song of the sea.'

The other two tenors told Blue that they would meet

him at the reception hall. Blue waved to them and directed his attention towards March again.

'Speak,' Blue said.

His voice was raspy and low – quite different from his singing voice.

March was nervous. 'Hi,' she said.

Blue smiled and showed his bright teeth. 'Hi. When do you sleep?'

'Never.'

'Sing. Sing me a song.'

There was no one left in the Auditorium. The lights inside had dimmed since the tenors had stopped singing. March sang. Blue tilted his head back and closed his eyes. He moved his cane in rhythm to the song. The lights started to brighten again. March stopped singing.

'Please. Continue.'

March started to sing again and this time, Blue sang along. The lights became brighter and brighter – they became so bright that the bulbs cracked and shattered and the floor was covered in glass. They both stopped singing.

'You have it,' Blue said. 'You have the voice of the world.'

'My parents said that I could sing since I was young,' March said.

'You're the one,' Blue said.

He put his hand on her shoulder.

'We will meet again some time,' Blue said. 'Whether in this world or another, we will meet again.'

Blue dusted the pieces of glass off his suit and limped away, leaning on his cane, nodding his head. He turned around.

'You will sing the sun to sleep one day and all will be well,' Blue said.

Because it was already morning, March left the Auditorium for the harbour to say bye to Fey and Fife. Walking by the café, she saw Mario through the window, serving a long line of customers. Morning was the busiest time of day for him and she recognized some of the customers from the Auditorium. Mario saw March through the window and waved. She waved back and asked a carriage driver if he would be kind enough to take her to the harbour.

'Beautiful morning today,' the driver said.

'I would like to think that it is a beautiful morning every day,' March replied.

The driver smiled and took her to the harbour. Fey and Fife were already there. They had to tie their hats around their heads because of the ocean breeze.

'We wondered where you were,' Fey said.

'I watched the three tenors sing throughout the night,' March said.

Fey had to board his ship. He hugged March and kissed her on the forehead.

'Don't be a stranger,' he said. 'You have my address; come over anytime. You will have a place to stay.'

Soon after, Fife had to board her ship.

'Just as Fey said, you will always have a place to stay with me.'

She kissed March on the forehead and walked toward her ship. March went home and started to clean up the house. After the death of the Armers, the house went to the next eldest of kin, which was Fey. He, in turn, gave the legal papers of the house over to Fife, who handed it over to March.

'It is your place,' Fife had said. 'Love it as it has loved you.'

Since the week of the Armers' burial service, March had been constantly busy – either with the funeral service, or with Fey and Fife. She now found herself completely alone in the house. She wanted to store the Armers' belongings in boxes and decided to begin with their bedroom. She stripped the bed sheets, the same ones that they had died on, folded them neatly, making sure that the creases were tightly made, and placed them in a box. They didn't have too much in their room. On one side of the bed was the dresser with a mirror. On the other side was a closet full of clothes. The two bedside tables each had matching bronze lamps. Each table also had a book that the Armers would read before falling sleep. March laughed out loud as she remembered Ons falling asleep with a book underneath his arms. When he woke up in the morning to kiss his wife hello, he would mistakenly kiss the book he was reading the night before. 'Too bad the book has no lips,' Sofi would say.

March placed the lamps in a box and wiped the dust off the bedside tables. The dust made her sneeze. She went to the dresser where all of Sofi's jewellery was kept in two small containers made of marble. On the outside were carvings of elephants. The one she opened was full of earrings and bracelets. Every one of them had some kind of blue jewel. March had never noticed that before. The other container had necklaces and rings, all of which had orange jewels.

'Like the sun and the ocean,' March said.

The dresser drawers had all of Sofi's clothes, the ones she wore regularly, including her nightgowns. She pulled out a few of the shirts and smelled the perfume. Its scent reminded her of watching Sofi dress up at night for an evening soiree – she would give March a little bit of the perfume. Of all the things the Armers left behind, she packed everything, except the perfume.

The most troublesome part of cleaning the Armers' bedroom was the closet, which was full of coats, dresses and suits. She took out three large boxes full of Sofi's dresses and, underneath the gowns, March saw a smaller container, opened, full of papers and envelopes.

'Love letters,' March said.

She assumed they were old letters that Sofi and Ons had exchanged. She was right, but there were also other letters – in these, she discovered a whole new world. She read some of the love letters first, realizing that the Armers, at one point, had lived passionate lives. This was a life she had never seen when she was living in their care. She looked at the dates of the letters and noticed that they were written well before Fey, Fife or herself were born. 'My Dear Earth' headed each letter written to Ons, in which Sofi would write about her feelings for him, which included the fact that he was the earth to her. The letters Ons addressed to Sofi began with 'My Dear Ocean', where he wrote about how she was the ocean to him and that he was just a seagull who flew above her. From the dates of the letters, she realized that they had been courting each other for nine years, from when they were both thirteen years old. From some of the letters, March discovered that their parents forbade their love.

'Like Shakespeare,' March said.

They had secretly loved each other for seven years without their parents' knowledge. The reason had nothing to do with politics or money – but rather, falcons and pride.

Ons's father, Perry, and Sofi's father, Lorenzo, were involved in falcon fighting. Perry and Lorenzo were the owners of the two best falcons in the falcon-fighting competition. In the championship tournament, Perry's male bird, Thunder, and Lorenzo's female bird, Lightning, were in the final round of the tournament. The match was anticipated to be one of the best fights of the falcon-fighting tournament. Pre-fight parties were held, bets were placed, street-lights lit up the town, as did fireworks and shooting stars. Thunder was considered to be the underdog of the two birds, though they were both equally fierce. As the bell rang, the two soared into the air to kill. But the unexpected took place and neither of the falcons won: once they were in the air, and as soon as Thunder was to make his first peck at Lightning, he fell in love with her. Lightning, who had once had the narrowest of eyes, looked at him with round, watery pupils. They fluttered in the air, in circular motion, observing each other's wings. As soon as Perry yelled 'fight', the two flew away together. Perry and Lorenzo never saw their birds again and they blamed each other.

'Your falcon is a womanizer!' Lorenzo screamed.

'Your falcon is promiscuous!' Perry replied.

They stood there for hours arguing about the fight and who should get the money. Perry claimed that he should since Lightning had followed Thunder. But Lorenzo asserted that since Lightning had followed Thunder, he should receive the reward money. The tournament judge, a Mr Shursh, ruled that they should split the prize money, but both refused, for each wanted all the money. So the town decided to use the money to buy drinks at Café Bar, while Perry and Lorenzo continued to squabble like chickens.

On that very day, Ons and Sofi met each other for the first time. Ons peered over his father's shoulder to see Sofi peering from behind her father's back. They stared into each other's eyes until they both felt dizzy and fell to the ground. Without saying a word to each other, they stood up and ran off to the field of orange trees where they discovered each other's bodies. They were cartographers. And while their fathers continued their dispute, while the rest of the town drank their brains away, Ons and Sofi realized the purposes of science and geometry.

Their parents never knew of their relationship until a few days before their respective deaths. Ons and Sofi told them, not out of guilt, but to let their parents know of their love for each other before they passed away.

It was awkward for March to think that Ons and Sofi had once lived a totally different life. She never saw them expressing any kind of physical intimacy while she was living with them. Perhaps the Armers were accustomed to hiding their love and so they did it for the rest of their lives.

In another box, March noticed a collection of envelopes and papers of a different tint. She saw that they were not love letters written between 'ocean' and 'earth', but letters written from a man named Jonas from the city of Kolkaper. She had never heard Ons or Sofi mention his name before. There was a huge bundle of letters tied with a red ribbon, which March carefully untied. When she saw who these letters were addressed to, her eyes widened and she started to breathe with such power that the letters before her fluttered around.

In his writings to March, Jonas had never mentioned that he was her father, or that Maria was her mother. He didn't know how to let her know, or when to let her know. Perhaps he hoped the Armers would tell her. Things had not gone as Jonas had planned. Maria and he would have moved to Koofay after they had saved enough money.

Then they would explain everything to March face to face. But Jonas did not think that doing it through a letter would have been respectful or effective. Each letter was addressed with 'My Dear Singing March'. He wrote to her as if he knew her as a good friend, as if he knew everything she did. March took the box out of the closet and sat on the Armers' mattress. The earliest date recorded was a letter written three weeks after she born. Jonas wrote about how Maria had been stabbed and was in a critical condition. He also wrote about how much they missed her. 'We loved to see you sing; we loved to see your eyes,' one line read. March sat on the Armers' bed and read letter after letter. She noticed that the later letters became shorter and shorter and that Jonas's tone was becoming sadder and sadder. March still didn't know who they were. She realized that she must have met them when she was a baby, but she wondered why the Armers' never told her about them. She worried about Maria, though she didn't know who she was, and she also worried about Jonas's condition, which was gradually declining as well. The last letter was the shortest, and the saddest: 'Dear March, I am about to forget you, but remember, Maria and I love you.'

March placed the letters back in their envelopes and then returned them to the box. She looked out the window as the sun reached its highest point. Her confusion was nowhere close to being cleared. She decided to visit Harnez, who was one of the Armers' few surviving close friends. He and his wife, Kayna, had known Sofi and Ons since they were all children.

Harnez's wife had died three years ago due to a broken leg. She didn't know that her leg was broken – she thought it was arthritis. Harnez told her to go see the doctor, but she refused.

'Doctors are for broken legs,' she told him.

On the morning of their fortieth anniversary, as Kayna stepped out of the bathtub on her broken leg, she fell and hit her head on the edge of the sink and died.

At her cremation, Harnez told Ons, 'She died clean and fresh. The less dirt on her, the less weight the wind will have to pull.'

Harnez had become a hermit since then. The last time he left the house was for the Armers' service and even then, he had sat in his wheelchair far away and hid behind trees. March walked down the street from her house to Harnez's house. The roof of his porch was supported by three small pillars, while the fourth pillar was broken and strewn in pieces about the ground. There were a dozen chickens in the front yard. The front door didn't have a handle, only a hole where the handle had been. March walked up the steps and knocked on the door. There was no response. She knocked again, louder and longer. She heard the squeaks of the wheelchair stop right on the other side of the door, but Harnez still didn't open it.

'Mr Harnez, it's March. Can I ask you some questions?'

The chickens in the front yard squawked in reply. March bent down and looked through the hole in the door. She saw Harnez's eye looking straight through the hole, causing March to jump back. She knocked again. Harnez opened the door.

'Don't let the chickens in,' he said. 'They are cranky.'

March looked around the living room. It was covered in dust. Near the window was a telescope, but March couldn't see the colour because of the dirt and mud that encased it. On a three-levelled shelf, she saw books with their spines torn or faded away. On the centre table was the doorknob of the front door. The walls were covered with old prints, including ones by Van Gogh and Munch. The room had no chairs.

'I am always sitting,' Harnez explained.

March sat on the floor and leant back against the wall.

'Why are you here?' Harnez asked.

His glasses, tinted dark, had slipped down the bridge of his nose. He wore a long-sleeved white shirt with faded blue stripes. It looked as if it hadn't been washed in days and was probably the only shirt he had worn for years. His brown pants were too short for his legs, revealing thin ankles. He wore black shoes with no socks.

'Excuse my attire,' he said. 'I haven't changed since the death of my wife.'

To March's surprise, he didn't smell badly.

'I still bathe,' Harnez said. 'And I wear the remains of my wife's perfumes.'

'Sorry to bother you,' March said. 'But I was wondering if you could help me understand something. I know you were close friends with my parents, Sofi and Ons Armer.'

Harnez bowed his head.

'I am their youngest child, March.'

'March,' Harnez said. 'I had seen you when you were the singing baby. My condolences to the family. They were loving people.'

'By any chance, would you know if I was born here, or in Kolkaper?'

The tea kettle from the kitchen whistled.

'Would you like some mango tea?' Harnez asked.

March accepted his offer. He came back with two cups and handed one to March.

'I love mango tea. When Kayna and I met for the first time at the café, we both drank mango tea.'

'My condolences to you,' March said.

Harnez did not reply.

'I know about your whole life,' he said. 'I'm probably the only person still living that knows about you, apart from Fey and Fife.'

March sipped her tea and let the scent drift into her nose and mouth.

'What do you mean?' she asked. 'Is it true that I was born in Kolkaper?'

'Yes.'

'Why didn't they tell me about this?'

'It's rather complicated,' Harnez said.

He sipped his tea, spilling some on his shirt. He didn't flinch and continued to drink from the cup.

'This tastes horrible,' he said. 'But it's the only taste I know.' He coughed. 'Though you can consider yourself an Armer, for they have brought you up since you were a baby, you are not an Armer.'

March placed her cup on the floor. Her stomach was rumbling, not out of hunger, but because of nervousness.

'You were the singing baby,' Harnez said. 'A baby who couldn't sleep and because of this, you had to leave Kolkaper.'

He ran his fingers around the spokes of the wheels.

'They wanted to take you away,' he said. 'The Armers agreed to take you in and become your parents.'

'Who wanted to take me away?' March asked.

'The Council, the townspeople, the scientists, everyone. They weren't sure if you would curse the town. They wanted to run tests on you.'

'So the Armers weren't my biological parents?'

Harnez did not reply.

'Who are Jonas and Maria?' March asked. 'Are they my real parents? I have found a box full of letters written to me by Jonas. Am I his daughter?'

Harnez looked into March's eyes. March looked back into Harnez's eyes. They sat there for eleven minutes, neither saying a word. The chickens outside continued to squawk in search of breadcrumbs. Harnez wheeled himself to a long string that was connected to the ceiling fan. He tugged on it and the fan began to rotate in a rickety movement. As it gradually moved faster, dust began to fall from the blades. The particles made Harnez sneeze. His eyes were red and watery.

'I can't remember when I last used this thing,' he said. 'Even the dust has died of old age.'

The rim of his collar was soaked with sweat. March wiped the perspiration from her forehead.

'I don't know who those people are,' Harnez said. 'Ons never told me who your parents are, but only your situation. And that your parents loved you enough to send you away for your own protection.'

'Did you hear anything about my real mother being stabbed?' March asked.

Harnez cleared his throat.

'I know nothing else about your parents.'

'Why did you call me the singing baby?' March asked.

'As soon as you were born, you started to sing, as if you had been singing for thirty years.'

He laughed and then coughed.

'And, as you know, you never slept. That is why they sent you away from Kolkaper. No one has ever seen a baby, straight out of a mother's womb, sing the song of the sea.'

'It is my favourite song,' March said.

'They were scared and wanted to send you away to the Cave Forest,' Harnez said. 'But your parents, they loved you too much to send you there.'

Harnez blinked repeatedly. March sipped her tea and tried hard not to make a face.

'You can't dream,' Harnez said. 'Pity.'

'What's the Cave Forest?' March asked.

'Kolkaper's outcasts reside there,' Harnez said. 'No one knows anything about them, other than that they are believed to be bad.'

'Am I bad?' March asked.

'Of course not,' Harnez said.

He spat out his tea and put the cup on the floor.

'What people don't know, they fear. They thought that you should go there and live among the outcasts.'

Harnez coughed and then took a deep breath.

'I must stop talking and rest. If I have helped you in any way, then I have helped you. If I have confused you, it is a confusing thing.'

March stood up and put the teacups on the kitchen counter.

'Thank you for your time,' she said. 'I wish you would leave the house more often.'

'There is nothing outside,' he replied. 'My next journey will be to meet Kayna. I am not good company, but come visit any time. I will die soon, though.'

March said goodbye to Harnez and Harnez gave her a loaf of bread to give to the chickens in the front yard.

That night, Harnez died in his sleep. He didn't struggle or have a painful death, but a simple one while dreaming of Kayna. The chickens cried throughout the night – they knew their friend had passed away. The next morning, the town woke up to the chickens' sobs coming from Harnez's yard. His neighbour, Lyle, walked over to his house and knocked on the door. The chickens were making him angry.

'Harnez,' Lyle shouted. 'Open the door, or they will be taken away!'

Not long after, the whole neighbourhood was at

Harnez's front door and when they didn't get any response, they opened the door to find him lying in bed, facing the ceiling with his eyes open. Lyle rounded up the chickens and took them to his house for safekeeping.

'My condolences,' Lyle said to them.

'Bock,' one of the chickens said.

After March visited Harnez, she went home and continued her packing. As she placed things in boxes of various sizes, she thought about Harnez's words. As night came, she heard the wail of the chickens from Harnez's house. She worked all night to finish boxing up the house. Her decision about the future was settled. She would travel to Kolkaper and look for Jonas and Maria, in the hope that they were still alive. She left for Harnez's house to tell him her plans and found that he had passed away the night before as his chickens cried. That evening was the cremation at the harbour. To the right of the service, a cargo ship was just entering the port. She looked to her left and saw Harnez's chickens quietly assembled for the service. One was wearing Harnez's glasses. But he did not know how far away he was from the edge of the harbour, for the prescription of Harnez's glasses did not match the chicken's vision. He fell off the harbour and into the ocean.

'He loved his friend too much,' Lyle said. 'Grief.'

After the service, March went to the café to see Mario. He was standing behind the counter, counting the number of lines on his palms. He didn't see March walk in.

'How many are there?' March asked.

Mario didn't look up. 'I'm not sure. I forget which lines I have counted and which ones I have not.'

He turned his head and saw March standing there. He immediately stopped what he was doing, pulled out a rag and began to clean the counters.

'I am leaving for Kolkaper soon,' March said.

'Why Kolkaper?' Mario asked.

'Do you think you can come with me?'

'I need a few more months to save money,' Mario said. 'You go and I will meet you there soon enough. Working in the café and the market, I should be able to save the money in no time.' He continued to clean the counter, making a squeaking noise each time he ran the cloth along the surface. 'Make sure to write to me once you are settled so I know exactly where to go.'

March nodded.

'I plan on going as soon as possible,' she said. 'I finished cleaning the house. Could you look after it while I am gone?'

Mario told her it would not be a problem at all.

'Maybe some day I can sell it and the money can be used for your travel,' March said.

'No,' Mario said. 'That house is where you grew up. You should try to keep it for as long as possible. One day, you may want to come back home and you will have one here waiting for you.'

March nodded. Both of them noticed that a long line of customers were standing behind March. She returned home and found two old suitcases and a small bag. In the small bag she found some new diapers, but she also noticed that they were an old style of diapers that were no longer in use. In it also were dried-up rose petals and a pair of gloves. It was this bag that Nirana had used when he took March to Koofay. March filled the two suitcases with clothes and the small boxes that contained Jonas's letters. In the small bag that had belonged to Nirana, she put in a few books to read while on the ship. It was late at night by the time she finished packing. She went back to the café where Mario was still working.

'I am leaving tomorrow.'

'It's about time. I'm tired of you coming to the café and holding up the line.'

They both laughed.

'Do you need help with anything?'

'I will be fine,' March said. 'I will take the carriage to the harbour.'

'I will look after your house for you and make sure that no one, including myself, steals anything. But please write to me and let me know how everything is.'

'I know,' March replied. 'I will write. And don't use your money on the trip because of me. You have worked hard for it. You do what you want to do with it.'

Mario looked down at the counter and began to wipe it. March noticed his eyes were watery and it made her own eyes water. Her feelings for Mario rushed to her head as they said farewell to each other. They hugged, but avoided looking into each other's eyes. Again, a long line of customers were waiting to be served.

'They can wait,' Mario said.

March walked out with her head down, trying not to let her emotions take over her body. She didn't understand this feeling and she didn't like it. She went back home and read until the sun rose. Then, luggage in hand, she locked the door and found a carriage waiting not too far from her house.

The carriage passed by the café on the way to the boats. March saw Mario walk out of the café.

'He works as hard as a baby trying to crawl for the first time,' March said.

She looked up at the sky and saw the grey clouds.

'Looks like the day will be wet,' the driver said.

March agreed.

'No matter,' he said. 'You will be surrounded by the ocean anyhow.'

She paid for the ticket and thanked the driver for his help. The ship departed soon after March boarded it. She had a cabin to herself for there were not too many people travelling that day. Pulling out a book, she began to read as the ship made its way out of the harbour.

Near the end of the trip, as March began her fourth book, stormy weather caused the ship to rock from side to side. March braced herself against the wall and placed her feet firmly on the floor to wait out the turbulence. She thought about sleep and how she couldn't close her eyes to dream. She thought about what Mario had said about sleeping – he was a strong advocate of slumber. When he wasn't working, he was sleeping.

'You can dream while sleeping,' Mario said. 'In dreams, you can live in another world.'

'But you have to wake up sooner or later,' March said.

'But sooner or later, you must also sleep.'

'But I can't.'

'It will come,' Mario said. 'And when it does, you will dream about me.'

March could hear the rain hitting the sides of the boat. The raindrops were large and heavy in the middle of the ocean. She heard a lady scream in the hallway. March opened the door and saw a lady running up and down the hallway shouting for help. A seagull was chasing her. The bird looked just as frightened, if not more, than the screaming lady. Seeing that March's door had opened, the bird flew into her cabin and March quickly shut the door. The flutter of its wings quieted. March said hello to the bird in a low soothing voice, so as not to stir up the chaotic flapping of its wings. The bird perched on the bench and looked about the room and then at March. The bird squawked and March squawked back. They sat there for five minutes squawking at each other until a knock on the door scared them both.

'Please open the door,' said a voice. 'We must get rid of the seabird.'

March said goodbye to the bird and opened the door, knowing that they would never be able to catch it. Now that it had been able to calm itself, the seagull fluttered down the hallway, up the stairwell and back into the sky.

The storm had stopped. March stepped out onto the deck. She saw the seagull flying away and gazed up at the grey-green sky. It was the first time March had stood on the deck of the ship. She looked around at the ocean that surrounded her. 'Where the ocean meets the sky,' she said to herself as she looked towards the horizon. She started to sing and immediately, the world began to slow down. The boat slowed down and started to tilt to one side. The seagulls slowed down, their wings barely moving and even the waves of the ocean were calmed. The captain came to the deck – it was Captain Don, the captain of the ship Nirana and March had sailed in from Kolkaper to Koofay.

'There is something familiar about you,' Captain Don said.

'I'm afraid I can't recognize you,' March said.

'Your voice,' Captain Don said. 'There was a voice once that sang the ocean to sleep.' He pointed to a dolphin, on its back, floating and sleeping.

'Please,' the captain said. 'Your voice is lovely, but we may not make it to Kolkaper if we all fall asleep.'

'Of course,' March said. 'My apologies.'

'No apologies necessary,' he said. 'The sun will set because of your voice and our troubles will sleep with it.'

The captain tipped his hat to her and went back inside to steer the boat. The salty smell of the sea made March hungry so she went inside to grab an orange and came back outside to enjoy her snack on the deck. She could see another storm coming and soon the boat began to rock violently again. The two captains on deck advised March to go back inside, where it would be much safer. As she was making her way back to the stairwell, she slipped on the wet floor. Just then, a huge wave tilted the boat. March fell off the ship. The captains didn't see her as they had already gone inside.

14

BENEATH THE SURFACE OF THE OCEAN, MARCH FELL asleep. Her eyes were closed and bubbles surrounded her nostrils. Her body reached the surface and she floated, her arms and legs bobbing up and down with the cresting of the waves. In her sleep, she saw flashes of Mario standing behind the counter, cleaning its top. She saw Mario walking towards her, smiling and talking, but she couldn't hear the words – she could only feel her skin tingling. She saw herself as a baby being held by a man she didn't recognize. She saw herself, again as a baby, cradled in the arms of a lady she didn't know. She saw a seagull with a man she didn't know in its beak.

March kept her eyes closed and without thinking, paddled her legs to propel herself through the water. She had never swum before, but her body worked instinctively. But every opportunity she had to get a good breath of air was swallowed by the stormy waves. Annoyed, she stayed beneath the surface and decided to learn how to swim with the dolphins around her – now was as good a time as any to learn, she thought. She opened her eyes and saw the Kolkaper port. March swam as much as she could towards the city; her legs tore through the ocean's body, her calves bulging. After using all her energy to swim underneath the surface, she rested and let the waves guide her towards the Kolkaper harbour. The storm had already passed over the city and the ocean was calm. She was not far from the shoreline. As March rested on the waves, she shouted 'Odysseus' and thought about Homer's poem. She was about to start swimming again when she heard someone say, 'Hello.' She looked around and saw a girl on a long slender yellow board.

'Are you okay?' she yelled.

'Just going for a swim,' March shouted.

The surfer was getting closer to her.

'I fell off the ship during the storm,' March said.

The surfer waded up to March and helped her onto the board.

'We should make it back in no time with the help of the waves,' the surfer said. 'You must be cold.'

'I dreamt,' March said.

The surfer looked back at the ship, which was still far behind.

'You swam from the ship?'

March coughed. The surfer laughed.

'You made it to Kolkaper quicker than the ship.'

'My legs helped me,' March said.

The sun began to show through the grey-green clouds, warming the back of March's neck. They made it to the banks of the shore and lay on the sand for a few minutes.

'Let's get dried up and then we can go to the harbour and wait for the ship to come with your belongings,' the girl said. 'My name is Kratoa.'

March introduced herself to Kratoa and thanked her again for her help.

'You would have made it anyway,' Kratoa said. 'I was just giving you some company.'

They walked on the sand towards a building that was used as a locker room.

'I have never walked on sand before,' March said.

'I wake up in the morning thinking of the sand,' Kratoa said.

'It feels like hot powder,' March said.

In the locker room, Kratoa and March dried themselves with towels.

'Rest,' Kratoa said. 'You must be exhausted.'

'I actually feel refreshed,' March said.

By the time the two had dried themselves and eaten at the beach café, the ship was in the harbour. March thanked Kratoa again for her help and they said goodbye to each other.

'You were a lifesaver,' March said.

'Not at all,' Kratoa replied.

She stopped and turned around to March.

'You're the lifesaver,' she said. 'I didn't know where I was. I was sleepwalking. It has happened to me before, but I have never gone into the ocean.'

'Sleep-swimming.' March said.

'When I woke up,' Kratoa said. 'I panicked. I thought I was going to die and the ocean was going to be my grave. Then I saw you swimming with the waves. It was then that I figured out where I was. We rescued each other from the water.'

'I am glad we were able to help each other.'

Kratoa sighed, waved to March and walked away. March walked towards the harbour. She recognized the captain who had warned her to stay away from the open deck.

'It was a tough storm, but the ship held still,' the captain said. 'It should be clear for the next stop.'

'It was my first trip on a ship,' March said. 'It wasn't too bad.'

March walked to her cabin and saw that, because of the storm, her belongings had been thrown about the place – but they were all there. She put her books and fruit back into her small bag, picked up her suitcases and left. The captain helped her with her luggage and soon after, she found a carriage driver.

'Beautiful horses,' she said to the driver.

'Thank you,' he replied. 'They have toiled on this earth since the earth was created. But they do not age, nor do they complain.'

'Would you know of any place where I can rent a room?' she asked.

'Of course,' he replied. 'I can take you there.'

The driver spoke to his horses and they began to trot away from the harbour onto the pathway that led to central Kolkaper.

'Have you heard of the Medallions?' the carriage driver asked.

March had heard that name before, but she could not remember where. She shook her head.

'The Medallions were the richest people in this town,' the driver said. 'They were philanthropists who kept this city alive and cultured. They have funded everything from the hospital to evening balls, to building hotels for visitors, such as yourself, to stay.'

'They sound wonderful,' March said.

'Never had a child though,' the driver said. 'They had one, but she sneezed soon after she was born and died of pneumonia. Since then, the city has become their daughter.'

'How sad and beautiful,' March said.

'Have you heard of the Faccinises?'

March's eyes widened. She figured out who the Medallions were. Jonas, in his letters, would talk about their grace and how they had helped Jonas and Maria. She remained calm.

'I have heard of the Faccinises,' March said. 'Tell me about them, please.'

She didn't want to sound too inquisitive or too

excited, just interested. She pretended she was a detective trying to solve a mystery, like Nancy Drew. The driver informed March about the life she never knew she had lived. He finished telling the story and a few minutes passed before March could say anything. She was trying her best to hide her emotions. She wanted to cry, she wanted to shout, she wanted to sleep – all at the same time – as she heard about her true parents.

'What happened to the Medallions and the Faccinises?' March asked.

'There is not much left of them all,' the driver replied. 'Both the Medallions just passed away, two days ago.'

The driver wiped tears from his face. His horse was crying too.

'Their funeral service is being held tomorrow,' he said. 'They died one day after the other. Nirana first, then Francesca. Both of them passed on in peace. They lived their lives like a well-stitched quilt, full of colourful patches.'

The carriage driver gave his horse a carrot to help soothe the sadness. He ate one himself and asked March if she would like one. She shook her head and asked him how the Medallions had died.

'Nirana died in the morning as he was drinking a cup of coffee. He took his first sip and then placed the cup down and walked to his bed to die. Francesca, the next morning, died as she cremated her husband. The fire burnt so bright, the light took away her last breath.'

March bowed her head.

'Conveniently,' the driver said. 'She was cremated right after her husband.'

An image of a ship and a man entered March's head – it was the same man that the seagull had held in its beak in her dream on the ocean bed.

'Here is the market where the tragedy took place,' the driver said, in reference to the Faccinises. 'The blood-stained dirt has finally blown away with the wind.'

As they drove past the market, March envisioned the stabbing that had taken place and created her own physical picture of their features in her head. It was the same man and woman who had appeared in her dream while she slept in the ocean – they were the people who held her and cradled her.

'How are they doing?' she asked.

'They are living and they are dead,' the driver said.

He explained that Jonas rarely moved away from Maria's bedside since the day of her stabbing. He had forgotten everything, including the Medallions, though they had visited him every day.

'Nirana told me one day that Jonas had forgotten to breathe causing him to almost die, but Nirana reminded him,' the driver said. 'Nirana had to pat him on the back to get him to cough and then he would remember to use his lungs.'

'And his wife?' March asked.

'His wife was remarkable,' the driver replied. 'She has been bedridden since the day of her stabbing some twenty years ago. But she has not shown any sign of ageing. She lies there with her eyes closed, a sleeping beauty she is.'

'Has she woken up at all?'

'No sign of her waking up,' the driver said. 'But every now and then, in the middle of the night, she wakes for only a few seconds to remind Jonas to take a bath, or tell him where his eyeglasses are, but she hasn't done that in a while.'

March took a carrot.

'When the Medallions were alive,' he said. 'They would come and help move Maria's body around to help keep her blood circulating.'

'But the Medallions are gone now.' March said. 'Will Jonas remember to do that?'

'It is a wonderful love that they have for each other,' the carriage driver said. 'When it comes to Maria, Jonas remembers everything he has to do to take care of her.'

As the driver finished his last sentence, they arrived at the hotel that had been built by the Medallions.

'I am sorry,' the driver said. 'I have talked too much. You must be exhausted. But we are here now.'

'No need to apologize,' March said. 'I should be thanking you.'

The driver helped March with her luggage and bade her farewell. Before he left, March asked him if he could be her driver while she stayed in Kolkaper.

'I will be your Kolkaper guide,' he said. 'A Virgil of some sort. My name is Thenly. Please settle yourself. I will have my lunch now and be back soon after.'

March walked through the lobby of the hotel. On the right, she saw paintings by Picasso hung on the wall. To the right of all the paintings hung a gold plate that said that these paintings had been donated by Francesca and Nirana Medallion and that each room had a Picasso painting given by the Medallions.

The hotel used to be the Medallion Mansion. When they moved out to live closer to Jonas and Maria, they made some extensions and turned the house into a place for tourists to lodge. Despite its extravagant decorations, such as the marble floors and walls, the glistening chandeliers and the silk-laced furniture, the Medallions vowed to never make it an expensive place to stay. They left Mr Thenly in charge in their wills. Mr Thenly took over the hotel, but also continued to be a carriage driver in his spare time.

'Being a carriage driver was my childhood dream,' he would tell his friends. 'I eat hay with the horses.'

MARCH PAID THE HOTEL CLERK FOR A WEEK'S STAY AND HE
showed her the way to her room. The door opened to a
short hallway with the bathroom on the right and straight
ahead were the living room and the bedroom. Over the
head of the bed, was Picasso's 'Old Man with a Guitar'.
Next to the bed was a closet and a dresser made of oak.
The living room had two pieces of silk-laced furniture.
There was a centre table with bronze legs and a glass top
that had been made when Kolkaper was just beginning
to grow as a city. Before metal studies became a crucial
part of Kolkaper's growth, glass making was one of its
premier industries and was headed by Lenea Galassier.
Coming from a wealthy French family, she was famous
for importing diamonds from Denmark and
transforming them into glass because the city of Kolkaper

seemed more interested in glass than diamonds. No one knew how she did it and Lenea never revealed her secret. With her death, the secret was buried with her and the only remains of her work are found in centre tables, chandeliers and other items of décor. The city believed that she came from the Cave Forest.

March thanked the hotel clerk for his help and lay on the bed for a few minutes before bathing herself. She left the hotel to see if Mr Thenly was waiting outside. He was there, talking to his horses.

'You look as refreshed as the morning dew,' Mr Thenly said.

March smiled and looked around her. 'Where can you take me?' she asked.

'There is a mourning dinner for the Medallions tonight at the banquet hall. Would you like to go?'

March nodded and they left for the banquet hall, which was not too far away.

'I could have walked,' March said.

'But who would give me company then?' Mr Thenly replied.

They both smiled. The place was crowded. The elite as well as the poor were mingling and talking about their memories of the Medallions. Also there were criminals whom Nirana had prosecuted and sent to jail. They were on special leave for the event.

'He sent me to prison,' one criminal said. 'But if I had to go, I wouldn't have it any other way.'

'The man was both sharp and kind,' another criminal

said. 'After he had successfully prosecuted me for my crime, he sent flowers to my wife.'

March followed Mr Thenly around the banquet hall.

'Will Jonas be here?' she asked.

'I doubt it,' Mr Thenly said. 'He is not a part of Kolkaper anymore, but only a citizen of his own mind.'

'Can you take me to his house?' she asked. 'I would like to meet him.'

'Of course,' he said. 'I don't think that he will give you good company, but perhaps a fresh face will wake him up a bit.'

He took a bite out of a piece of celery covered in peanut butter.

'If you are looking for some kind of work,' Mr Thenly said, 'you can take care of Jonas and Maria. The Medallions asked me to find someone to take care of the Faccinises in their wills.'

'I'm training to become a doctor,' March said.

'This will be a good start,' he replied.

March accepted the offer. They left the banquet hall and went to the Faccinises' house – it was covered in vines and she couldn't see the house's colours. Next to it was the Medallions' house with lit candles on the porch. The front yard of the Faccinises' home had two trees, and their branches jutted into the house. One of the branches went straight through the front window. March could see a bird's nest on one of the branches in the kitchen.

'No need to knock,' Mr Thenly said. 'He won't answer.

Just walk in. I'll wait outside. He has long forgotten who I am.'

'Even though you saved his life?' March asked.

'Sometimes I wonder if I really did save his life,' he said.

March walked inside. All the rooms were dark. She heard the birds in the kitchen. She walked down the hallway and into the living room. It was well kept because the Medallions had taken care of this house as long as they were alive. From the living room, another hallway led to two bedrooms on opposite sides. She noticed the door on the right had a faint light coming from it – she peered inside. The first thing she saw was Maria lying in her bed. Her eyes were closed and her arms were placed by her side. She looked young.

'A swan's grace,' March whispered.

She walked inside the room and bowed her head. A cough from the corner of the room startled her. She saw in the shadowed corner a man sitting in a rocking chair. Jonas didn't know that March was in the room. His eyeglasses were on the floor near his feet. He was rocking back and forth in his chair with his head tilted to a side as it rested on his hand. His body odour tickled March's nose. The room smelled of stale onions, which made March's eyes water.

'Jonas,' March said.

Jonas didn't reply; he continued to rock in his chair. His eyes were closed. The chair squeaked in perfect rhythm. March cleared her voice and called his name again. The chair stopped rocking, but his eyes were still closed.

'I am here to take care of you and Maria,' March said. 'I have been hired to help take care of you and the house.'

He started to rock in his chair – and there was squeaking again. He spoke in a weak, thin voice.

'I hear the birds singing in my head,' Jonas said.

Those were his first words since he had spoken to Maria fourteen months ago, when he told her that her nose was still pretty.

'They're in the kitchen,' March replied.

'I can't see my glasses,' Jonas said. 'But I wonder if my glasses can see me.'

'They're on the ground. Right next to your feet.'

'Where are my feet?'

'They are attached to your legs.'

'And my legs?'

'Attached to your body.'

The chair stopped rocking. Jonas ran his hands along his own body, as if he were trying to figure out whether he existed or not. He tapped his feet against the floor. He sat still for a few seconds and then picked up his glasses and put them on.

'There I am,' Jonas said.

He looked at March.

'I have seen those eyes before,' Jonas said.

She turned her face and looked at Maria. March didn't see any signs of breathing, yet she looked vibrant for the state that she was in. Her skin was tan rather than pale. Her eyebrows were prim and her toenails were cut perfectly around the skin.

'How is she?' March asked.

'I have seen those eyes,' Jonas said. 'I remember those eyes.'

He looked at Maria.

'She has been resting now for twenty years,' Jonas said. 'Soon she will wake up.'

March was still standing at the doorway of the room. She wanted to tell him that she was his daughter.

'I will be back in the morning,' March said. 'I will get some sleep now and see you and Maria tomorrow.'

'Sleep?' Jonas replied.

'I will get ready to take care of you all,' March said.

Jonas nodded. March went outside to where Mr Thenly was waiting. He was talking to his horses.

'Would you like to go back to the hotel?' he asked.

March didn't say anything – they made their way back to the Medallion Hotel.

'I do not know your name,' Mr Thenly said.

'March.'

Mr Thenly stopped the carriage in the middle of the path. The horse listened to a nearby owl. His eyes were large and round as he turned to March. Her eyes were just as wide. She could hear her heart beating inside her ribcage. The driver looked at March's eyes, studying them. He gathered his composure and told his horses to start trotting again.

'You are the singing baby,' Mr Thenly said. 'The baby who couldn't sleep. The love of the Faccinises and the Medallions.'

'I have come to Kolkaper to find my biological parents,' March said. 'I learnt about them through the letters Jonas had sent. I found them after my parents in Koofay passed away.'

'My condolences,' the driver said. 'And what do you plan on doing, now that you are here and have seen them?'

'I will look after them as long as I am here,' she said. 'I don't know much about them, but I know they loved me, because they sent me off to live a good life.'

She looked at the trees on the side of the road. She felt the vibrations of the carriage as the horse's hooves hit the cobbled road. All of it seemed familiar to her.

'I feel that my mother was stabbed because of me,' March said. 'And now I want to take care of them. I want to take care of them as they would have taken care of me.'

THE NEXT MORNING, MARCH WROTE MARIO A LETTER, TELLING him her situation and where she was living. She told him about her real parents and how her carriage driver was the same as the man who had been the carriage driver of the Medallions and the Faccinises. She told him about how she had been a baby who could sing from the day of her birth and how they wanted to send her to the Cave Forest. Mr Thenly took her to the post office.

'If you don't mind, I think I will walk around for a bit before seeing my father.'

'I will wait here,' Mr Thenly said.

Around the corner from the post office was a small market. She walked by and looked at the jewellery and clothing. In one section of the market, there was a small stall, the smallest of them all, and March saw a child advertising skirts of earthy colours. He had no customers yet, but stood there, waiting for whoever would come.

'Cover your body with these skirts,' he shouted. 'All colours. All sizes.'

'Hello, little boy,' March said.

'Do you like these colours?' the boy asked.

He picked up a dark green skirt made of silk and handed it to her.

'I like it,' she said.

'Would you like to buy it?' he asked.

'Not now,' March said.

The boy shrugged.

'But I will definitely come by later,' March said. 'Are you open every morning?'

'Only once a week.' the boy said.

He looked at the ground and began to lightly kick the dirt with his shoes full of holes.

'Where did you get these skirts from?' she asked.

'I made them,' he said.

He looked at her. She could see the pride in his eyes mixed with despair.

'Are you from here?' March asked.

As the boy was about to reply, a man from the other side of the market started to shout at him.

'No outcastes allowed in the market,' he said. 'Go back to the darkness of the Forest.'

The man ran towards him, but his weight slowed him down. This gave the boy time to quickly gather his skirts and place them in a bag. Without looking at March, he started to run away. A few seconds later, he ran back to March and handed her the dark-green skirt.

'I made this for you,' he said. 'Take it.'

He ran off again before March could say anything. The man, who was shouting at the boy, eventually arrived. He was breathing hard – his moustache was drenched in sweat.

'They should stay in the Forest and never come out,' he said. 'They do not deserve the sun.'

'He is from the Cave Forest?' she asked.

'They don't belong here,' he said

'Why is the Forest considered such a bad place?' March asked.

'It is a world full of oddities,' the man said. 'Too strange. Too many defects.'

'I think you're just scared,' March said.

The man looked at her with narrowed eyes. The sweat from his moustache dripped to the ground, forming a small puddle. He walked away.

March went back to the carriage with the skirt in her hand and told Mr Thenly about the incident in the market.

'Nice skirt,' Mr Thenly said.

'I love it,' March agreed.

'It is full of talent,' Mr Thenly said. 'Exquisite.'

'I must come back and pay him,' she said.

They started off for Jonas's house. On their way there, as March bought some food to take to Jonas, she asked Mr Thenly if he believed that the Cave Forest was a bad place.

'They are perhaps talented and misunderstood,' he said. 'I am in no position to judge others.'

When they arrived at the house, the birds in the kitchen had left for the day.

'They must be running errands,' March said.

Mr Thenly waited outside while March went in to see Jonas, who was sitting on the chair that March had first seen him in. His eyes were open and he had his glasses on.

'And you are?' Jonas asked.

'I am here to take care of you and Maria,' March said.

'I remember those eyes,' he said. 'I used to hold you when you were a baby. Maria too. You were the singing baby. The baby who never slept.'

'Some things haven't changed,' March said.

She felt her stomach rumbling with nervousness. But Jonas didn't tell her that he was her father or that Maria was her mother. March was not sure that Jonas remembered that she was his daughter – only that they used to hold her when she was a baby.

'You ran away from us because we were going to send you to the Cave Forest,' Jonas said. 'We were scared of you and now you are back to curse us.'

He had a coughing spasm.

'Not true,' March said. Her voice quivered.

The room was only lit by the sunlight coming through the window. Jonas sat in the corner where it was dark.

'You sent me off to Koofay so that the others would not send me to the Cave Forest. You sent me away out of love, not fear. I am back to take care of both of you.'

Jonas turned his face to the floor. He rocked his chair, which squeaked every time it went back.

'You and Maria are my parents,' March said. 'Don't you remember?'

Jonas stopped rocking the chair. He continued to stare at the floor. Turning towards Maria, he asked, 'Maria, is this our daughter? Do we remember?'

Maria remained motionless. But before Jonas spoke again, she opened her mouth.

'March,' she said. 'From our crib.'

And that was it. She didn't say anything else. March went up to her, but she didn't move. It was as if nothing had ever happened.

'How can she speak?' March asked.

'She does that from time to time,' Jonas said. 'To make sure my head doesn't fall off.'

Jonas looked up at the ceiling fan.

'We are your parents,' he said. 'I know that. But you ran away because of the Forest.'

March realized that Jonas was mixing up different stories.

'You had strong lungs, strong eyes,' Jonas said. 'And so you went away.'

March, who was still standing, looked down at her legs and noticed that they were shaking. The sunlight made Jonas's eyeglasses sparkle despite the dust on them. She sat on the floor facing Jonas.

'Please remember,' March said. 'You loved me and took care of me. And you didn't want me to go to the Forest so you sent me to Koofay to live with the Armers.'

Then March changed the subject. 'You need to eat or else you will die like a street dog that only has its own bones to eat.'

'I have forgotten how to eat,' Jonas said.

'All you have to do is chew and swallow,' she said.

She took out a small bowl of rice from a brown bag and walked up to Jonas. Being close to him, March saw the skin on his bones sagging; his white button-up shirt was covered in dirt and grime, making it look black, rather than white. It barely clung to his body. The smell of his onion-scented body made March's eyes water. She turned towards Maria and smelled roses – the scent of her body had not changed since the day she was stabbed. March scooped up a few grains of rice and put the spoon near Jonas's mouth.

'Open your mouth, please,' March said.

Jonas turned his face away from the spoon and looked at Maria. March jumped back as Maria spoke. Her eyes didn't open. Her voice was strong.

'Jonas,' Maria said. 'Eat. Or your eyes will fall out.'

Jonas turned his head to March and opened his mouth. March gently put the spoon into his mouth. She saw his black gums; his teeth had holes. Once the grains were in his mouth, March told him to start chewing and then to swallow. Jonas did as he was told and March continued to spoon-feed him.

'How come she still talks as if she is awake?' March asked again.

Jonas finished chewing his rice.

'She lives in a world between life and death,' he said. 'Between the ocean and the sky, she exists. Every now and then, she will tune in to the living world.'

Jonas opened his mouth again and March fed him some baby carrots.

'Do you think she will ever be truly alive again?' she asked.

'She is on her way,' Jonas said. 'She's leaving this world.'

'How will you know when she is gone?' March asked.

'When I die,' he said.

'When was the last time you bathed and cleaned your teeth?' March asked.

The birds were back in the kitchen. March and Jonas could hear them chirping in their nest.

'I have forgotten how to bathe,' Jonas said.

'You are in bad shape,' March said. 'You must clean yourself. Let me help you.'

Jonas agreed to bathe, but he would not leave Maria's bedside. March found a large, tin tub and filled it with hot water. In the bathroom, she found soap, which the Medallions had given him as a gift.

Jonas got up from the chair and walked to the tub. He didn't take his clothes off. March laughed. She took off his shirt and pants and told him to sit in the tub. The bin was just big enough to fit him. He had to scrunch his knees to fit properly. March used the rag and soap to bathe her father. Layers and layers of dirt and skin fell off, revealing a fresh skin.

'Like a snake,' March said.

Jonas remembered the feeling of bathing. He remembered that, years ago, every morning he would wake up and bathe before going to work.

'The morning cleansing of the soul,' he said.

After she finished cleaning his body, she brought him a clean pair of pants and a fresh white shirt that had not moved from his closet in years. He had forgotten how to put on his pants, so March helped him one leg at a time. After that, she buttoned his shirt.

'One more thing,' she said. 'You must clean your gums and teeth.'

Jonas opened his mouth to show his teeth and March scrubbed them with a toothbrush.

'It tickles,' Jonas said. 'I will laugh.'

After she had finished cleaning him, Jonas looked at Maria and then at the floor. He laughed.

'What is it?' she asked.

'Ah yes,' Jonas said.

March placed the glasses on his face.

'Today is my birthday,' Jonas said. 'And you are our daughter.'

For the first time, March saw him smile, revealing his shiny white teeth.

'And we loved you with all our might,' Jonas continued. 'And that is why we sent you away, so they would not scorn you and send you to live in the Forest.'

He nodded his head.

'Yes,' he said. 'You are March, the baby who sang from Maria's womb.'

'You remember,' March said.

'It came to me all of a sudden,' Jonas said. 'Probably from Maria somehow.'

Jonas yawned.

'All that bathing has made me tired,' he said. 'I will go back to my chair and nap.'

March told him that she would leave the house and get something to eat and that she would be back in the evening.

'I will bring you dinner,' she said. 'Gradually your appetite will grow again.'

'I'm afraid I'll be gone soon,' Jonas said. 'But while we are all here, let us enjoy each other's company.'

March left the house to see Mr Thenly waiting outside. He had a sandwich in one hand and he fed apples to his horse with the other. He was just taking his last bite as March walked up to the carriage.

'The sun is on its way down,' he said.

'I think I will go for a walk,' March said. 'You should take the rest of the day off. I think I will only go back and forth between the hotel and the house. I should be okay.'

'If you do need me,' Mr Thenly said, 'just ask the hotel clerk for my whereabouts. He will know.'

Mr Thenly rode away. March walked around the corner to see another small market. It was similar to the one she had been to. March was not accustomed to seeing a market on almost every other block, because Koofay had only one market. She walked around and looked at the fruits, jewellery, clothes and walking canes. In a corner, March saw a child selling clothes. She recognized the boy from the other market. Again, no one was at his stall and he just stood there and looked at the people as they walked by.

'You didn't let me pay you for the skirt,' March said.

The boy's face was covered with dirt. March handed him some coins, but the boy put up his hands and refused.

'No,' he said. 'It is a gift from me.'

'But it looks like I am your only customer,' March said and grinned.

'But my best customer,' the boy said, grinning back.

'So you make all these yourself?' March asked.

'That I do,' the boy replied. 'I learnt how to stitch and make clothes when I was a baby. But since I am from the Forest, no one will buy my clothes.'

'I think they're beautiful,' March said. 'Be patient. People will eventually see the talent in your eyes.'

She crouched down and kissed him on the cheek. The boy shyly slid his right foot across the dirt and looked up at her.

'Thank you,' he said.

'Thank you for the skirt,' March said. 'I will wear it for a beautiful occasion and everyone will be wondering where I got such a skirt. I must leave now and attend the Medallion funeral service.'

'Yes,' the boy said. 'The Medallions are travelling today.'

'You know of them?' March asked.

'Yes. They were among the few from Kolkaper who actually cared about those who lived in the Cave Forest. Mr Nirana tried to get rid the barrier between the Forest and the city, but the Council would not have it.'

March began to walk away, but then stopped and turned around. 'What is your name?'

'Raj,' he replied.

'Raj,' she said. 'I am March.'

Raj nodded, his huge smile never waning. March laughed to herself as she walked away. She thought that it was cute that such a young boy had such charm. She asked a nearby carriage driver for a ride to the harbour. When she arrived, she saw a large number of people there. Night-time was approaching and the harbour was lit by candles held by those at the funeral service. She saw Mr Thenly in front of the crowd. It was the first time March had seen him with a solemn face. Next to Mr Thenly, to her surprise, were Jonas and Maria. Jonas was sitting in the same rocking chair that was his room and Maria was lying on the same bed. Mr Thenly had helped them get to the service.

'They should be there,' Mr Thenly said. 'The Faccinises are their ghosts.'

March slid through the crowd up to the front where they were. Jonas, who was staring into the ocean, glanced at March. He remembered that she was his daughter. He tugged on her arm and March bent down to his face.

'Who's the service for?' he asked.

'The Medallions,' she whispered.

'Who?' Jonas asked.

'The Medallions,' she said. 'They helped you take care of Maria and they helped you and Maria to send me off to Koofay.'

Jonas nodded.

'And with a sneeze,' he said. 'She was gone.'

He began to rock the chair back and forth. Mr Thenly placed his arm underneath Jonas's and helped him stand up.

'They have chosen you to release their ashes into the ocean,' Mr Thenly said.

He placed the urn in Jonas's hands and helped him walk towards the edge of the cliff. As he was about to throw it into the ocean, a seagull came and took the urn from Jonas's hands with its talons. With one big yelp, the seagull flew away. The crowd, in awe, began to murmur.

'What happened to the Medallions?' Jonas asked.

'The seagull took them away,' Mr Thenly said.

March noticed that Mr Thenly wasn't distressed or agitated. After a few minutes, the service ended and the people walked away.

'You don't seem worried about the urn being taken away by the seagull,' March said.

They both walked towards the carriage.

'It is all a circle,' he replied.

'A circle?' March asked.

'Not too many people know this,' Mr Thenly said. 'Perhaps only their closest friends – the Medallions were not born in Kolkaper.'

Mr Thenly went on to say that no one knew where they came from, or who their parents were. A seagull had brought both of them over in a basket. One day Nirana came and the day after, Francesca followed. They came from nowhere. His father had found Nirana on the doorstep and Francesca had landed in the Forest.

'And what about Francesca?' March asked. 'No one cared that she was from the Forest and lived in the city?'

'Most people would worry about it,' Mr Thenly said. 'But they didn't know that she was from the Forest.'

They stopped at the carriage and faced each other.

'I was born in the Cave Forest and lived there for some time,' Mr Thenly said. March found out that his mother, Bornea, and his father, Pangaea, secretly loved each other. They would travel in the night, either to the Forest, where his mother lived, or to his father's house in Kolkaper. After the seagull dropped her off, Francesca was brought to the house of his mother's neighbour and that's where she lived.

There was a cool wind. March's hair fluttered around her face. She tucked it behind her ears.

'I was not born yet,' he continued. 'So whenever my mother and father rendezvoused in the Forest, Nirana would go to the neighbour's house and play with Francesca.'

Mr Thenly put his hand on top of his hat to keep it from flying away.

'By the time they were five years of age, Nirana and Francesca had fallen in love with each other and vowed that they would marry when they were sixteen.'

'And so it is a full circle?'

'They came and went with the seagulls.'

'But how did everything work out – if everyone was living in secrecy?' March asked.

'My father told everyone that Nirana was a friend's son, visiting from overseas,' Mr Thenly said. 'One night in winter, my father snuck my mother, Francesca and me from the Forest and into Kolkaper.'

'Did anyone notice?'

'When people asked who they were, my father would reply that they came in with the North Wind and left it at that.'

'But I thought that the Medallions were rich people who came from a long line of wealth,' March said.

'My parents were the wealthiest in the city of Kolkaper,' Mr Thenly said. 'But no one knew it. My father loved being a carriage driver and mother rarely thought about money, only about her love for her husband.'

He told March that in their will, they had left him all of their money, but also entrusted him with the care of the Medallions.

'And I did,' Mr Thenly said. 'I supported them until Nirana was able to work. He worked hard and became successful. And soon enough, they became the wealthiest in the city.'

'What about you?' March asked.

'I drive these two beautiful horses around. That is all I need.'

While he talked, Mr Thenly had driven all around the town, until finally they found themselves at the Faccinises' house.

'Have you ever gone back to the Cave Forest?' March asked.

Mr Thenly nodded. 'People here think that those from the Forest want to come to the city and live here and take over the city. It's quite the opposite.'

'How so?'

'The Forest is a beautiful place,' Mr Thenly said. 'It's a world of its own, and its citizens don't want anything to do with Kolkaper, except perhaps to make amends.'

As they got out of the carriage, March saw Raj hiding behind the bushes of the house.

'What are you doing here?' March asked.

Raj walked out from behind the bush, with that familiar smile on his face. He looked at Mr Thenly and continued to smile. Mr Thenly patted his back.

'You know him?'

'He is my connection to the Forest.'

'How so?'

'He is my son – he lives with my wife, who lives in the Forest.'

March looked at Raj and then at Mr Thenly and noticed the similarity in their facial features, especially their eyes.

'I have decided to carry on the tradition of my parents – bearing love that is as secret as a thief's belongings.'

'Will they ever move here?' March asked.

'Raj wants to continue to sell his skirts, and then someday become a brilliant mayor of the Forest who will bring Kolkaper and the Cave together,' Mr Thenly said. 'And that way love will have no boundaries. Go home, Raj. It is getting late, Mother will worry.'

'I have a new idea,' Raj said. 'Sunglasses. I will make sunglasses. People will wear them over their eyes, so they won't have to squint in the sun.'

Raj hugged his father's leg, and kissed March's hand.

'Very charming,' March said.

Raj ran off.

'He will make a great husband and father one day,' Mr Thenly said. 'Go now and see how Jonas and Maria are doing. I will wait outside.'

March told him that he need not wait and that she would walk home. They said goodbye and March went into the house. For the first time, all the lights in the house were on. The birds were sleeping in the kitchen. March could hear Jonas's chair rocking. His room was the only one without a light. March walked in and turned the light on. Jonas was in his chair and Maria was in her bed.

'Hello, Father,' March said.

Jonas opened his eyes and smiled. His glasses were on his face.

'Good evening,' he said.

'A beautiful service, earlier today,' she said.

'There was a service today?' Jonas asked.

March had to remind him about the Medallion funeral service that they had gone to earlier that day and how the seagull came and took the urn away.

'The seagull,' Jonas said. 'I thought it was the sky's hand that took it away into the ocean.'

Jonas continued to rock in his chair. She could tell that Jonas was not feeling too well. He was breathing hard and his eyes were barely open.

'Father,' March said. 'You only have one shoe on.'

'I forget these things,' he replied. 'I am a lost life now.'

He turned and looked at Maria. 'Maria has passed now. She is gone from this place.'

March looked at Maria. She looked the same as before.

'How do you know?' she asked.

'She told me she was going,' he replied. 'And I am not too far behind.'

March bowed her head.

'I never knew her,' March said.

Without opening his eyes, Jonas spoke, 'If you know yourself, you will know her. You two are two bodies with one soul.'

The birds in the kitchen woke up and started to chirp.

'Ah yes,' Jonas said. 'It is time for me to go. I remembered to love you, March. Take care of yourself. And now I must remember to die.'

He drew his last breath and his head tilted down. His

chair continued to rock back and forth. March closed her eyes. She walked up to the chair and stopped it from rocking. She moved Maria to the side and placed Jonas next to her on the bed. Curious about the rocking chair, she sat on Jonas's throne.

'Comfortable,' she said.

She pretended that she was asleep on the chair and thought about Mario walking towards her. She thought about the ocean and the sky and giraffes. She thought about the Armers. She pretended that she was dreaming.

The next morning, March told Mr Thenly of the news and they contacted the funeral home to start preparing for the service. The service was held four hours later. It was a small one, with only March, Mr Thenly and the birds from the kitchen.

'A great journey,' Mr Thenly said.

It was a short service and then the Faccinises were no longer.

ON THE NIGHT OF JONAS AND MARIA'S FUNERAL, A STRANGE
occurrence took place. The sun never went down. The
citizens of Kolkaper stood on the doorsteps of their
houses, waiting for night to arrive. Their legs became
weary and so they sat on the doorsteps and waited. The
sun showed no signs of departing.

'Go sun,' one citizen said. 'Go away.'

'Stubborn light,' another said.

The inhabitants didn't know what to do – this had
never happened before. Some stores accidently stayed
open longer than usual because they thought it was still
afternoon and not night. The children were excited
because they weren't told to go to bed. 'How can we
send them off to bed?' one parent asked. 'The sun is
beaming through the curtains like lightning.'

The stray dogs and cats all looked up with their tails raised and their tongues out, wondering when the streets would be dark and quiet and ready for their lurking. The crickets, wanting so badly to chirp, couldn't be a nuisance – they too were confused.

It was now midnight and the citizens were becoming cranky and grumpy. No one was nice to each other. No one could really even speak anymore. They were either scared or shocked; no one was amused. Around one in the morning, there was an impromptu town meeting at the Centre Square. Here, Rinja and the Council discussed with the citizens what they ought to do.

'We can cover the town with a huge blanket,' one person said.

'Is there a way we can all go temporarily blind?' another asked.

'If I can't sleep,' one citizen said. 'How will I be able to water my plants in the morning?'

There was disorder and constant bursts of outrage and frustration. Rinja was at a loss.

'This must be the doing of the Forest,' someone shouted.

'Forest,' Rinja whispered to himself.

He hurried off without saying a word to the rest of the Council – and they were left arguing with the townspeople.

March sat in the kitchen of the Faccinises' house and enjoyed the stubborn sun. Four days had passed since Jonas and Maria's funeral. Four days had passed since the sun had refused to go away. The problem of not being able to sleep wasn't new to her, nor a hassle. There was a knock on the door and when she opened it, she saw two aged men with long grey beards. They each wore tattered top hats and held splintered canes. Their lab coats had holes in them and the sleeves were unravelling as the threads had become loose. Their spectacles had broken flames and each set of glasses was missing a glass. They looked at each other and then at March.

'We are Larry and Rezna,' they said.

'Which one is Larry and which one is Rezna?' March asked.

They pointed at each other and said the other's name.

'And what can I do for your?' March asked.

'It has been too long,' Rezna said.

'Times have changed,' Larry said. 'People have changed.'

'Do I know you?' March asked.

'I know you,' Rezna said.

'I know you,' Larry said.

'We know you,' they said at the same time.

'We are scientists,' Larry said.

'I should be afraid of you,' March said. 'No matter. You can't do anything now, being as aged as crocodiles.'

'We come with good intentions,' Rezna said. 'Rinja, the head of the Council, has sent us here.'

'Just like the first time,' Larry said.

'But this time, we are humbled beggars,' Rezna said. 'And not myopic enemies.'

March invited them in. They went to the kitchen, where she offered tea to the ragged-looking scientists. They politely said no, as their nerves, their health, were not in good shape due to the lack of night and rest.

'We now know the life you live,' Larry said.

'We now have seen the world through your eyes,' Rezna said.

'A lot has changed since we held you in our arms so long ago,' they said at the same time.

'Help,' Larry said.

'Us,' Rezna said.

'Please,' they said at the same time.

The scientists and Rinja had met, discussing possible ways of making the sun go down and they believed that March would be the best chance to rid the town of this curse. Rinja knew where this trouble came from.

'It is a curse from Jonas and Maria,' he had said to the scientists. 'With their deaths, they have left a parting gift – a gift of scorn.'

The scientists agreed.

'We deserve it,' they all said. 'We must be forgiven. We must correct our faults.'

Both Larry and Rezna had stepped forward, saying they would approach March because they were the ones who had acted as a catalyst for the Faccinises' demise and March's departure to Koofay.

'So here we are now,' Larry said to March.

'Will you help us?' Rezna said.

March looked at the nest, resting on two branches

that were jutting into the kitchen. She looked at the tea kettle on the stove and a painting of Jonas and Maria on the wall next to the cupboard.

'Meet me at the market in three hours,' March said.

'When the sun is supposed to set,' Rezna said.

The two scientists each put one of their hands on March's shoulder. They bowed their heads and remained speechless. It was their way of saying thank you.

MARCH FELT GLORIOUS. SHE STOOD AT THE MARKET, LOOKING at the sun, she felt something inside, a spectacular sensation she hadn't felt before. There were only three other people there – Rinja and the two scientists. They stood a few feet away from her and faced the sun. March wore a long white gown; it was Maria's wedding dress. There was a strong wind coming from the ocean and the dress fluttered in the wind, making her look like some kind of beautiful ghost. She didn't acknowledge the three men's presence, but stared at the sun with her head slightly tilting to the side. She was in a daze – she was awake and dreaming. When the spectacular feeling and the glorious sensation inside of her was in perfect harmony with the world, she opened her mouth. This was her enlightenment.

My dear world,
this is the song of the sea,
listen with your eyes closed,
listen with your lonely sighs,
and let this voice carry you away.

This is the song of the sea,
sad and soothing,
let it carry you away
to where the world turns
and reverses itself to another time.

My dear world,
this is the song of the sea,
listen with your eyes closed,
listen with your lonely sighs,
and let this voice carry you away.

Oh ocean, oh birds,
wave and chirp and hear me now,
we will sleep and dream
and we will let ourselves go.

My dear world,
this is the song of the sea,
listen with your eyes closed,
listen with your lonely sighs,
and let this voice carry you away.

Come on moon, come on sun,
this is the sad song of the sea,
lift your heads and rest your chins,
and let my voice guide you to your pillows,
we will all feel better in the morning.

My dear world,
this is the song of the sea,
listen with your eyes closed,
listen with your lonely sighs,
and let this voice carry you away.
Together, all, we will travel and see,
from one land to another,
from one sea to a new horizon,
and there will be adventure and love,
and there will be a new life for us all.

My dear world,
this is the song of the sea,
listen with your eyes closed,
listen with your lonely sighs,
and let this voice carry you away.

March sang the song of the sea eight times before the
sun started to move. Rinja and the two scientists had
fallen asleep standing. They had already closed their
eyes during the second song. The whole town was asleep
as March's voice boomed through Kolkaper. It was the
loudest March had sung – she used all of her might. She
used every muscle in her body and her lungs were

performing at full capacity, even beyond full capacity. Her voice was strong enough to sing the sun to sleep. It looked tired as it went down, almost drooping over itself – just as the three men's heads were drooping over their shoulders. March kept singing and night came, and the town was dark. The stars came out and shone brightly because there were no clouds to cover them.

March tapped Rinja's shoulder. Rinja tapped Larry's shoulder. Larry tapped Rezna's shoulder. They were all awake. They looked for the sun, but it was gone. They all smiled and turned to March.

'We are forever grateful,' Rinja said.

'Kolkaper can now sleep again,' March said.

Larry and Rezna each put one of their hands on March's shoulder and bowed their heads.

'You're welcome,' March said.

'I am sorry,' Larry said.

'I am sorry,' Rezna said.

March turned to Rinja.

'There will be no more tests,' March said. 'And children will not be taken away from their parents.'

The two scientists nodded their heads.

'Never again,' Rinja said. 'We have made mistakes and we now understand the importance of variety – of what we don't know or aren't accustomed to.'

'The Cave Forest will no longer be a cave,' March said. 'It will be respected. It will be welcomed.'

'We completely agree,' Rinja said. 'There's much to be learnt and no longer will Cave Forest be shunned.'

The three men went back to their homes. March walked back to the Faccinises' house. She lay in bed and closed her eyes. It was the first time she felt exhausted, but as soon as she closed her eyes, they opened again. She realized that this would be her life – a life where her eyes would always be open except when they blinked.

THE MORNING AFTER THE SUN HAD GONE DOWN, MARCH bathed and then went for a walk around Kolkaper. The townspeople all greeted and welcomed her. Some hugged her, others shook her hand or gave her gifts. They all thanked her.

'This morning I woke up and my hair was all messed up and I smiled,' one person said.

'My morning tea felt like morning tea,' another said.

'I was late to work today and it was great,' said another.

'Thank you,' they all said together.

March kept walking and found herself heading for the Forest. As she arrived at the edge of it, she saw Raj standing there. He ran to her and grabbed her hand.

'Welcome,' he said.

They walked through the Forest until they reached the centre, where March saw a whole new world. The trees were oak and willow and sycamore. Their branches were decorated with shiny ornaments, causing the Forest to sparkle and from this sparkle, music was made – it hummed throughout.

'Just like another town,' Raj said.

There were markets, houses and offices. People walked to and fro, going about their daily business.

As they walked into the town, she saw the talents of Cave Forest. A small girl in the market was creating beautiful furniture. A baby, who was in a small cradle, was making a candle.

'He can't talk,' Raj said. 'But he's great with wax.'

March felt comfortable in the Cave Forest. She couldn't understand why the people of Kolkaper thought this was a place to be shunned. She thought that it was quite the opposite.

'This is all so beautiful,' she said.

On that same day, March decided to live in the Forest.

IT TOOK MARCH FOUR MONTHS TO MOVE TO AND SETTLE IN the Forest. She built a house with the help of Raj and the girl who could make furniture. Mr Thenly helped too. On the dresser in her room, she kept the box of letters written by Jonas. There was also a photograph of the Armers and next to it was a bronze bangle and a pack of diapers.

She became a biology teacher for the younger students at the local school, while practising to become a doctor. She wanted to open her own practice, not only for the Forest, but for people from across the world. She also coached football teams and helped children deal with their nightmares. From time to time, she would visit Kolkaper, for she still took care of the Faccinises' house, where the bird family still lived in the kitchen.

Mr Thenly's wife, Bornea, passed away happily, while making toast for breakfast. He and his wife never lived together in Kolkaper – because they did not want to. They were too accustomed to loving each other in secrecy and they kept it that way. Bornea died with a smile as she thought about her son. Raj was on his way to becoming quite a successful businessman. His skirts sold throughout the world and his sunglasses were becoming more and more popular. He was also a part of the Forest Council, the youngest member, and he had made strong connections with Kolkaper – so strong that the citizens of Kolkaper would visit the markets of Cave Forest and Kolkaper would welcome the inhabitants of Cave Forest with no hesitation. The two lands blended with each other and there was no longer any enmity between the Forest and Kolkaper.

The Forest also gained one more inhabitant. Without telling March, Mario went to Kolkaper in search of her. After years of selling oranges in the market and cleaning the countertop at the café, he had saved enough money to move. Mr Thenly, in the final days of driving his carriage, took him around and showed him the city. He knew he was going to die soon, because his wife had recently passed away.

'Lovers,' he said. 'We must go hand in hand – just like the seagull and the urn.' On the last day of his life, he told Mario where March was living. 'Travel to Cave Forest. There, in the centre of the city, you will find the ocean meeting the sky.'

His last breath drew his carriage to a stop. Mr Thenly died without any wrinkles on his skin. His horses would mourn for him for a week by refraining from eating carrots. Mario went to the Forest to take Mr Thenly home to his son and to find March. He found Raj's office and told him of his father's death.

'This is good grief,' Raj said.

He thanked Mario and turned back to his father, who lay on the office desk.

'My father,' Raj said. 'Thank you for your kindness and these veins of mine.'

Before he left, Mario asked him if he knew where March was staying.

'A good season for oranges,' Raj said.

He found the market and saw March buying oranges. She had dropped a few of them and was crawling on the ground to pick them up. Mario walked up to her, but so engaged was she in picking up the oranges that March didn't see him.

'Hello,' Mario said.

He started to sing to her. March looked up and felt the goosebumps on the inside of her skin.

ACKNOWLEDGEMENTS

Thank You: Mommy and Daddy and Deep, Andy Breaux, Stacey and Terry and Charlie and Ada Grow, Lindsey and Luke and Audrey and Sam Sonnier, Rien Fertel, Katie and Denny Culbert, Bianca and Chad Cosby, Angelique and Brandon Sonnier, Casae Hobbs, Karl Schott, Ryan Castle, Eddie Barry, Clare Maraist, Anu Gupta, Erin Bass, Jeff Distefano, Justin Bacqué, Mark Chaisson, Tori Anders, Patrick O'Neil, Kristin Stoner, Ryan Dilbert, Andrea Pappas, Jennifer Ames, Mark Maynard, Tupac Shakur, Red Ink Literary Agency, Anuj Bahri, Sharvani Pandit and Ajitha G.S.